The Secret Daughter

About the Author

L. C. Davis spent her early life in rural New Jersey, where creative writing, music, and art created the foundation for a life in the arts. While studying opera in college, she became fascinated with the personal lives of the composers. As she honed a successful career in the corporate and non-profit worlds, L. C. devoted her spare time to writing short stories and penning her debut novel, *The Secret Daughter*. She is a member of the Women's Fiction Writers Association and the Author's Guild.

L. C. Davis

The Secret Daughter

Vanguard Press

Dedication

For Laura, my love and light.

Acknowledgments

To Tannis, without whom this book may never have been written. To Laura and Ryan, with love. There are many more whose support and good humor kept this story alive. I am forever grateful to you all.

Chapter One

The faint smell of cigar smoke lingers like ghosts on the upper floors of the Palace Library of Budapest. As Marie climbs the ornately carved wood staircase, a sense of dread slithers up her spine like a dark eel. Libraries have always been her haven, her happy place of peace and solace. This library feels markedly different.

The third floor is much darker and colder than the floors below. An oversized book sticking out from a shelf diverts Marie's attention. As she reaches for it, a man with a black hat obscuring his face appears from the shadows. He grabs the book, slips something inside, and shoves it toward Marie. He disappears in the darkness behind the shelves.

"Wait, who are you?"

Marie's entire body is shivering. She tightens the fleece scarf around her neck; *Creepy*, she says under her breath. She abandons her search for a book on eighteenth century harpsichords, and heads down to the first floor; a more inviting space where students hovered over textbooks and small groups chatted quietly. In a cozy nook by a heater, she settles in to open the mystery book. A rectangular envelope falls out. Inside is a smaller envelope and a note, scrawled on a ripped piece of paper. It reads:

Now, you are the keeper, die Wächter. *Be true to his wish, forever!*

Marie opens the smaller envelope; the sepia-colored paper is transparent like onionskin. Inside are two letters. Marie carefully lifts them out. She reads the first one.

January 15, 1818

Cold seeps through my clothes and my heart, for I can never be warm without my body enveloping yours as I have done precious few times, my love. I grow older, deafer, and sullener. Why do you wait so long to visit me? I love you though you torment me so.

Forever yours,

LVB

The second letter, a reply, two days later:

January 17, 1818

My love, ordinary days keep us apart, and my aunt, having been exposed to the worst of the fever, lies close to death as I write. It is her clinging to life that keeps me here. Oh, how I wish she would take in her final breath so, I would be free! Fly to you on the fastest horse in the land. I dream it every night.

Forget not how my warm body responds to your touch, your healing, life-giving touch. My love, my master, you will have me again, and I shall beg you never to stop.

Hold fast, my love, I am coming to you.

Yours

Marie's heart is racing, *I recognize this; the entwined letters on the red wax seal, and the signature, "L.V.B." as in Ludwig Van Beethoven.* Her first instinct is to hide them. She carefully puts the letters and note into her bag, which she now holds tight to her chest. *It can't be real.* Beethoven's letters have all been published many times over. But these letters, the dates, the intimate exchange, she'd never seen anything like this before. The note, the strange man, what did it all mean? And most puzzling of all, who was the note from, who was simply, "Yours?"

Marie's mind churned. Every classical musician, Marie included, knew Beethoven's love story, a tragic tale of forbidden love. But, supposedly, only one love letter was ever found, yet each of these letters appear to be from Beethoven to his Immortal Beloved. Given no choice, they kept their affair secret; a small pearl of truth held just between Beethoven and his lover. If the press got hold of the letters, judgements and theories would fly around social media. Their relationship would be cheapened and diminished. No, Marie would not be party to that. If the letters are legitimate evidence of his secret affair, she'll keep them hidden, at least for now. In his time, the world was not kind to Beethoven, why would it be so now? Her heart wept for them; everyone deserves a private life, and if Beethoven and his lover wanted their affair hidden from the world, then Marie would not betray them.

Still, she couldn't ignore the tingling in her spine, the pang in her gut. If the letters are authentic, it upends everything we think we know about Beethoven, and his music. It could rewrite the history of classical music entirely. Marie reviewed the historical facts. The one Immortal Beloved letter found among Beethoven's things documented and on record, is dated 1812, but these letters were written five years after that, and a year after the Broadwood pianoforte was sent to Beethoven.

The 1817 Broadwood pianoforte, Marie's insides shivered. Just hours ago, she had played it, one of the most magnificent pianos in history. She was one of only three piano technicians to ever work on the historical instrument. In fact, since Beethoven died, only a handful of pianists have played it in almost two centuries. A thought crosses Marie's mind: if the letters are real, the only "soul" to have witnessed the truth of his affair is the piano.

Afternoon turned to evening as Marie sits clutching her messenger bag, hardly moving except for her eyes which darted left and right, fearful the man from the third floor might return. Could the letters be a hoax, but why and why were they given to her? The library lights dimmed; a soft chime sounded to signal closing time. She texts her driver and gathers her things. She puts her messenger bag on first and her coat over it. She wants to keep the letters as close to her as possible.

It was later than usual when she arrived back at the winery B&B, her home in Budapest for the next few weeks. The lights in the great room are on and there's a note on the table.

"I put a plate in the oven for you. Sleep well, Tilda."

Well, that's a surprise, Tilda, the manager of the B&B, has a sharp edge to her which makes Marie wary.

She pecks at Marie about her work. Every day the same questions, "What did Braun say?", "Is the piano ready, how much longer?" It's annoying, but it's the way Tilda looks at Marie that unnerves her most. Marie is careful to be as cordial as possible, but her gut warns, Tilda despises her. Why Tilda would despise her is anyone's guess. It might simply be because of who Marie is; an American woman working on one of Hungary's greatest treasures. A plate in the oven, an unexpected kindness. Maybe, she is warming to Marie after all.

Juggling the plate and her bag, Marie fishes the room key out of her pocket, but it drops on the floor. That's when she notices the door has been forced open, her room ransacked. Her clothes have been yanked off the hangers, thrown in heaps on the floor, her nightstand is on its side, the drawers and contents strewn across the room. *Oh, my God, who did this?* Marie runs to find Tilda; she, or someone else must have heard something.

Marie can hear Tilda's snoring through the door. She hesitates. Why would Tilda go to bed if she knows Marie's room had been ransacked? It doesn't make sense; most likely Tilda knows nothing. She decides not to wake her. Tilda's moods are unpredictable, and the last thing Marie needs is to get into an argument. She remembers her messenger bag upstairs. Marie ran through the great room and flew up the stairs. She immediately went for her bag on the desk and opened it. The letters are still inside. Then it dawned on her. Maybe, whoever ransacked her room was looking for the letters. Why else would they search through all her things? Her aunt Evangeline's gold watch, which she had forgotten to put on this morning, sat on the desk untouched. Clearly, this wasn't a robbery. They were looking for something specific. If they were looking for the letters then that's one question answered, the letters are not a hoax. That fact is enough to rattle anyone who has studied Beethoven and especially Marie. The connection can't be a coincidence. The only reason she is in Budapest is to tune Beethoven's 1817 pianoforte, you can't get much more connected to Beethoven's story than that. Is that why the strange man in the library gave her the letters; does he know she is working on the Broadwood? Marie's head is spinning with more questions than answers. But her focus, for now, must be her safety.

Whomever ransacked her room was long gone, but Marie's adrenaline is still pumping. Seeing her clothes strewn across the room makes her shudder. To think someone else's hands had touched her things. *It's scary but, I'm OK. I'm not the first tourist to get robbed in Budapest.* Mustering her practical side, Marie tries to focus on what comes next; laundry, first on her list in the morning, check; get Tilda to replace the lock, check. She put on her aunt's gold watch, next item on the list, where she would sleep tonight; certainly not in her room with the state it's in now, and a broken lock on the door. She grabbed her pillow and messenger bag and headed to the couch in the great room. If someone tried to harm her tonight, they'd have to do it in the center of the B&B where everyone would hear.

Chapter Two

I am frozen in time against my will, enduring being moved and cared for like the relic I am since my master died. For over two hundred years I have been in this lifeless, whitewashed corner of a square room I detest. I am placed by a large window which pleases me and disgusts me on any given day. The putrid color of the synthetic fabric curtains, they part just enough to let the light warm my wood, the rosewood and oak polished to an unnatural sheen on my sides. I am not placed with purpose, I am wedged between a plain wall, and Franz Liszt's memorabilia, how dare they!

I am the great 1817 Broadwood fortepiano made expressly for Beethoven, the greatest maestro of all time, yet I sit cloistered here in a dead museum. Breathing the manufactured air, biding my time, I remain untouched like the town's wretched spinster. The room is soulless in its box-like shape, the carpet cheap and rough as sandpaper under my purposeful feet and pedals. My lid cannot soar upward, instead it retreats in fear from the low ceiling, which is unnaturally flat and dull, not made to carry sound, but to thwart it!

I tolerate the glint from Liszt's swords in that glass box permanently locked in place too close to me. His portrait stares down at me yet betrays the light he carried in his soul, layer upon layer of oil paint the smell still sickens me as it wafts over my frame. The blue in his eyes is not his. Even I know Liszt had the piercing dark eyes of an artist, one who sees beyond the ordinary. The muted thud of the machine which pumps frigid air into the room, laughs and curses me with its incessant off-pitch whistling and whining.

In the evening, I feel the museum exhale when all the lumbering people have gone. The room glows from the impossibly small lights along the floorboards of every wall. Even Liszt's artifacts sleep and leave me in peace. In these hours, I can still smell her lilac perfume and hear the lyrical rise and fall of her voice. She loved me as she loved Beethoven, she knew my worth, she knew I would serve Beethoven and her until they chopped me into firewood.

Soon, they will move me again; my own room where I can be alone with this young Marie. Beethoven and I will not rest until our story is told, until his letters are safe again in the arms of his love. It's time to tell our story, a story I cannot keep locked inside my wooden heart any longer.

This young woman, our Marie, she must hear me!

***

The door to the piano room is heavy like the soundproof door in a radio station. When Maire shuts it, she feels insulated, protected. She exhales and begins to relax. Tilda promised to replace the lock on her door right away and

18

hopefully, there would be no more break ins at the B&B. Putting last night's incident aside, she turned her mind to her work. The piano must have more to say. Today, she will coax it into trusting her, see if she can woo it into allowing her to play it and most of all, communicate with her again.

Sitting at the Broadwood, its formidable presence is visceral like déjà vu only much stronger; Marie *knows* this piano. She has a connection to it, no matter how absurd it seems to her rational mind. It may be only the second time she is in its presence, but somehow, she is familiar with the piano. She knows the keyboard, her body sits at just the right angle on the bench, her feet find the wooden pedals intuitively, and yet, she's never played a piano with wooden pedals before. Marie silently talks to the piano as if it's an old friend. She's talked to grand pianos before, it's not out of the ordinary for her, but there is something else. When she talks to this piano, she can feel it responding. She can feel it… listening to her, emphasising with her. It's a two-way conversation even if it happens in the language of silence.

Marie reminds herself not to get too caught up in the piano's history or it's longing. She has a habit of becoming attached to pianos she doesn't own. Getting too close to the Broadwood, a piano she will most likely never see again once her work is finished, would be a mistake. This opportunity is a feather in her cap, the first assignment she's had in years with this kind of notoriety; it could help propel her career. The validation and the money aren't bad either. *It's just pieces of wood and wires, s*he repeats to herself, *just like every other piano*.

The keys wait like obedient children for her to command them. The Broadwood, so different from any piano Marie was sent to tune, modern or vintage instruments. Designed expressly for Beethoven, with the latest technology of the time, it is indeed unique; English action with six octaves, the first piano made with a stabilizer bar. Anyone who had the great fortune to play it, even today, was privy to an extraordinary experience.

But it is delicate, like a child's bones, wood, and wire nonetheless, but Marie hesitated as if she might be scolded for touching it. She straightened her back and reminded herself she was paid to be here as she was one of very few people in the world trusted to touch this magnificent piano. Her heart is racing, anticipating the whole, rounded bell sound she would hear. Triple wire strings, deer skin hammers not felt, and the small, condensed body that seemed defiant in its petite frame.

She caressed the white keys, then the black, carefully getting to know the keyboard, the scratches in the ivory, the spaces and the depth of the keys, their short length. Her small fingers seemed designed to fit them perfectly. She took in the smell of the instrument, earthy, deep tones of rosewood and oak, the scent of lemon oil used to polish its utterly sensual body. The wood glowed under her gaze, warm butterscotch tones, glints of gold, like bolts of shimmering satin unfolding without yielding around her.

She held her breath, letting her right-hand fall into a Major C triad. The sound was almost as she imagined, less rounded, and slightly staccato. She played a simple melody carefully feeling her way through the shortened finish of each note. The chord endings boxed themselves in like naughty children in straight-backed chairs. It took a few minutes for her to perfect the amount of pressure she applied to the keys, at first too much, too loud to allow the full expression of the sound to finally, softened ballet-like graceful bends of her wrists produced the fluid tones she imagined.

She plays the woeful Moonlight Sonata moving gently as the music carries her away to that place pianists go where no other human exists, and they are one with vibrations in the wood, the warm ivory keys, and the stretching and yearning of the strings as the hammers hit, interrupting the breathless pauses.

Lost in the music, her head remains tilted upward as she finishes the piece, drinking in the last falling echoes of the notes. She is in awe of the sound, with how at home the music feels being evoked from this piano—the very piano on which it was composed. The resonance between Marie and the piano is a welcome comfort, every cell in her body is humming. She hasn't felt this serene and at peace since her dear Aunt Evangeline died.

She checks her phone, seven p.m.; later than she thought. The museum is dark except for a light in one of the offices. Just then, Braun, the Museum Director, enters the room. Marie is surprised to see him.

"I'm sorry I kept you so late, Braun, I didn't realize the time."

"Not a concern for me, but perhaps the piano could use a rest."

"Fool!"

Marie heard the word, a loud whisper coming from behind Braun. She waited for recognition from him, but he seemed completely nonplussed.

"Did you say something?"

"No, I believe you heard me, yes?"

"Yes, sorry, Braun. I'll be leaving then."

Braun stared at Marie, his body squarely in front of her, his presence filling the room. It unnerved Marie, but she couldn't bring herself to look away.

The limo ride back to the winery is slow, the streets of Budapest crowded, but Marie doesn't mind. She thinks about what just happened in the piano room when Braun came in. She heard the piano speak, didn't she? It clearly said, "fool," it must have been referring to Braun, but why? Braun did not react, but maybe, it's because he didn't hear it. If the piano spoke to her, it didn't scare her, but instead, it intrigued her. Marie has always been unconventional and in truth, it wouldn't be the first time she heard the woeful longings of a grand piano. It was curious why this piano, Beethoven's piano, over two hundred years old, chose to speak to her. Hopefully, given some time, she would come to find out.

Inside the soundproof limo, she watched the lights from the cars whizzing by in the bustling city, cafés filled with couples, the theatre marquee lights, and the blinking streetlights created a silent symphony of life humming around her. Marie watched the world from a distance, just as she always had. Her heart was not lonely, but it was filled with longing.

Her childhood was solitary with both her parents absent even when they were at home which wasn't often. Becoming a classical pianist and eventually a piano technician was a solo endeavor, hours of practicing, composing, and studying. While her classmates in grammar school were gluing paper hearts and candies on pink and red cards for Valentine's Day, Marie was at the piano practicing scales and simple works by Mozart and Brahms. By fifth grade, invitations to parties and skiing, or the local pool in summer had stopped coming. Marie Vuillard was not a social girl the other mothers would say, she's a musician.

Her own mother gave her very little in the way of encouragement or affection. She dutifully reminded her of her lessons and recitals and shooed Marie out the door to the waiting taxi or her Aunt Evangeline, who never missed one of her performances. Her mother did not attend her recitals, she never took Marie out shopping or for lunch, and there were no girl's day outings or movies. It was Aunt Evangeline who bought Marie her first recital dress. Her father, a science professor at Harvard was a phantom figure in her life. She saw him sporadically when he happened to be home for the holidays or when he and her mother took the day off to pack for yet another research trip. The only constant in her life was her grand piano, a seven-foot Steinway grand, sequestered in a faraway room on the third floor of their Beacon Hill house.

The piano welcomed Marie in the early hours before school or in the dark of midnight. She could play as loud as she pleased, no one could hear her in heavily insulated room on the top floor. In summer, she would open the large windows and play as the sunshine dappled the lid of the shiny black Steinway, dust particles dancing in the breeze. Marie imagined she was playing in a garden, a concert for the birds and the foxes running between the impossibly manicured lawns and shrubs.

Marie remembers a particular bright fall day when she took the long way home from school to sit on a bench by the Charles River. Crimson and orange leaves whipped in wind as she watched children jump in leaf piles, mothers scolding them for losing their hats. The smell of apple cider, the orange and purple Halloween lights made Marie smile. The Vuillard's never decorated their porch for Halloween and shut the porch light off before dinner, better not to encourage the neigborhood children from incessantly ringing the doorbell, chanting, "Trick or Treat" in an obnoxious pitch. At thirteen years old, Marie had never worn a Halloween costume and never joined the neigborhood kids to trick or treat. She wondered what it would be like to be someone else, just for a few hours. One autumn afternoon, her aunt Evangeline decided it was time Marie experienced "normal kid things." She overheard her arguing with her mother in the kitchen.

"She needs to experience life Meg, real life, like other kids. You can't keep her locked up in this mausoleum her whole life. If you don't want to do it, then let me."

It seemed to Marie her mother gave in too easily. She liked winding Evangeline up, and she seemed to jump at the chance to have Marie out of her hair. Her mother agreed Evangeline could take Marie trick or treating. Meg also agreed to let Marie stay at Evangeline's house on a more extended basis. Marie was happy, she loved her aunt, but the sting of knowing her own parents did not miss her, hit hard, even if it was buried deep inside.

Evangeline had a piano, an older Steinway in excellent condition. She gave Marie everything she needed to make it her own. She could practice and play, whenever she chose, even if it was two in the morning. Evangeline was like that; a free spirit, a nonconformist and she loved Marie deeply. Marie's life began to change when she stayed with Evangeline, long-term. At first, she was a little shy. Evangeline talked nonstop at the dinner table and offered Marie the chance to taste wine and champagne. She encouraged Marie to talk about her dreams and her fears. It was hard at first, dinners on Beacon Hill were silent, her parents hardly spoke to each other and usually never talked to Marie. Confirming dates of holiday school closures, final exams, these were the critical topics of conversation. Sometimes, no one spoke at all. It took Marie a few weeks to let down her guard.

"But I don't have anything to say aunt, not really. I went to school, I practiced, that's it."

"What did you play? What do you love playing, what do you hate playing? Do you love your mother's meatloaf, I mean really Marie, just tell me anything!"

"You know she doesn't cook. Carlotta makes the meatloaf, she knows I love spicy food, so it tastes like tacos, mama hates it!"

Evangeline erupted into laughter and Marie could not help, but laugh, too. Within a few months, Marie and Evangeline were like two peas in a pod, they finished each other's sentences and dinner time became Marie's favorite time of day. They would cook together, make garlic bread, set the table with mismatched China and linen, laugh, and even talk with their mouths full at the table.

Marie eyes mist with every memory of Evangeline. Those memories seem to come so often these days.

***

In the great room at the Tordas winery, the large fireplace is blazing. Tilda the house manager had laid a place for Marie at the table even though everyone else had long since moved on to their evening plans after supper promptly at six p.m. She called out for her, and Tilda came bustling in her usual harried manner.

"Hello and good evening, Miss Marie, a good day at the museum, I hope."

"Yes, another good day, an interesting day, but I'm famished, thank you, Tilda."

"Ah, no thanks needed." Tilda served Marie and sat opposite her at the family-style long wood table.

"So, tell me what was interesting about today? Did Braun smile?"

"Ha, no, I think that would be too much to hope for. No, it was the piano. It… ah, it will sound crazy, never mind."

"Crazy, no, interesting (using Marie's word again). What do you mean?"

Tilda's English was fair enough, but Marie thought sometimes Tilda pretended not to understand just to get her talking. Tilda loved Beethoven, and she loved the history of the 1817 Broadwood. She wanted to know everything Marie did, down to the most minute detail of her work. It was a bit intrusive, and Marie found her constant pecking annoying.

"Well, many times in my work, I can feel a sense of the piano, like the people who played it, the sadness and the joy the instrument experienced. But today, well, I could swear I heard it actually speak a word."

"What word?"

"Fool."

"Ah, is Braun, yes?"

"Maybe, but still, it's crazy, right?"

"I don't thinks it's crazy. That piano, has a soul."

Tilda got up and went into the kitchen. Marie sat for a while thinking about what Tilda said. Tilda was right the Broadwood had a soul, a soul filled with yearning and Marie wanted to know more, she wanted to know everything it would tell her. She had cautioned herself not to get too close to it, but now, she thought it was impossible for her not to do so. Being in Budapest felt right somehow, a place she never imagined she would visit. Now that she is here, it feels like she is in the right place at the right time—probably for the first time in her life—Marie felt she was where she is meant to be. Whatever else Hungary had in store for her, she would accept it and see this through. The piano, Beethoven's piano, Marie, still couldn't believe she was playing it and especially, that it chose her to communicate with; how could she ignore it? Marie downs the last sip of wine in her glass and yawns, she's bone tired and needs to rest. Tilda shows her the new lock on the door to her room, a double lock no less, how thoughtful. Within minutes, she's asleep.

The next day Marie leaves for the museum early to get in some extra time with the piano, playing it, but also listening to it. If it was the Broadwood that spoke to her last night, she wanted to know why and what else it had to say.

Braun greeted her with his usual icy handshake, escorted her to the piano room, and walked away without saying a word. Inside the chilly temperature-controlled room, she wrangled herself free from her scarf, hat, coat, and messenger bag, laid them on the desk, and went to the piano. She stroked its side. "What have you got to say to me today, my lovely," she purred.

She carefully opened the lid and placed the wood support in place. Fully open, the piano seemed to inhabit the entire room. She bent over it peering at the inside and stopped. She heard a faint whisper again. She waited for what might come next, staring at the insides of the mighty instrument. Restoration from many years ago blended with more recent work. Initials of the piano technicians who went before her scrawled on the wood. *The inside of the piano is truly the most fascinating*, she thought. She heard it again.

"I don't understand what you want perhaps you could be more plain, sir."

She heard footsteps, the stiff purposeful thud of Braun's gait. They were eye to eye, yet she found herself staring at Braun's crease-pressed jeans, and shoes.

"Yes?" she said.

Braun's shoes, she stifled a laugh, *uptight and stiff,* she thought. The highly polished black Italian leather with military-like buckles made her think his shoes mirrored his taught manner. But then she noticed his thigh muscles slightly bulging out of his crisp black jeans, and it excited her. On second thought, maybe, Braun's shoes are modern and sexy; it made Braun seem dangerous and interesting despite what Tilda said. Braun shifted his weight and Marie watched his muscular legs take a wider stance, feet shoulder width apart.

"Is everything all right?"

"Yes, of course. I am looking at the restoration that's been done over the years. Fascinating."

Marie did not move from the piano. Instead, her mind drifted to the poetry of the piano's body, the details of the meticulous work of piano technicians before her, the history of the Broadwood's life and Beethoven's life, absorbed into the grain of the wood, even the nail heads nestled in for posterity.

Braun didn't move.

"I'm sorry Braun, did you need to talk to me?"

Silence.

"No, just checking on you. Enjoy your day, Miss Marie."

Braun left and Marie had to laugh a little. She sensed his attraction for her, but she doubted he knew what to do about it. It would be fun to see if ever actually acted on it.

Marie sat down on the bench, flexing her fingers, and taking a few deep breaths. Today, she will test it. Fur Elise first, an easy piece, then something more complex like Opus 132, if she could manage to play at least some of it, she'd know what the piano was capable of. Let's see…

She plays softly at first then becomes lost in the music. The piano is singing. To Marie, it feels as if they are one head, hand, and heart. The instrument knows her phrasing even though this was the first time she played through a piece of music. Like two people on a swing, moving in tandem, feeling the ebb and flow of flying up and down, up, and down, pumping harder to see how high you can go. Marie lost all concept of time and place. Breathing the music, feeling it pulse in her veins, filling her lungs, and releasing through her hands. Her mind meanders to the letters, Beethoven, and his secret lover how brave and bold they were. The music recanting their story, the chords demanding mezzo-forte, then forte, telling her their love was intense and real. She is sweating and panting, feeling the pain and ecstasy of forbidden love that prevailed over everything in its way.

Release me, release me!

The piano spoke to her, and she obliged playing the song over and over until she could no longer move her fingers. Her mind is racing, mesmerized as the piano talks to her. The piano was clear—it wanted her.

I feel her heart skip beats as my Therese Marie's did so many years ago. She is like her in many ways, even though these modern times are so different. Her face, lovely in the light, her body, long and lithe, and her eyes are weeping even when she is smiling. To possess her would be a great conquest, no doubt. Luring her to me, I am commanding her to embrace me, her warm skin on my wood. Come closer, dear Marie, I need you!

The piano has needs, Marie had no doubt of this. It wasn't the first time she heard a piano speak to her. Especially, antique pianos which hold echoes of music and of the artist who composed at its keys. Energy, passion, love, these things are not so easily dissipated, but clearly, this piano was extraordinary, and her suspicions of it specifically needing to communicate with her were confirmed. There can be no mistake, this piano was masculine in its energy. Marie is wary of men with great needs, and she recognized his need, but she didn't acknowledge it right away. She is curious as to what it holds inside and what it needs to release, but she must try to remain in control.

Marie's heart is beating so fast she can hardly breathe. She stops playing and walks away from the piano. Putting distance between herself and the intense need of the spirit inside the piano felt like the right thing to do in this moment. She downs a glass of water, takes three long deep breaths.

"OK, you've got my attention now, trust me, I trust you."

There was someone else in the room. She waited, her hands on the side of the piano, her back turned to the door.

He came closer, whispered into her hair, "I will not harm you; I need you, give yourself to me."

It's Braun, and this realization made her want him more. This seemingly stoic man who looks her straight in the eye, his crisply pressed jeans, Italian leather shoes with military-like buckles, obviously, there is more to him and the fact that he allows his passion to drive him excites her. Most of Marie's past relationships were brief—fleeting might be a better word. Men got close too quickly in her opinion, they didn't know her, they didn't care to know her, they were chasing an ideal. Each one had their own mixed-up notion of what their ideal woman was. Usually, it meant someone who was subservient, but interesting, men want spark, a woman with a bit of sass. Trouble is, they want the sass to come with a remote so they can turn it on and off to suit their mood. Sex is something Marie needs in her life. Sex has its place, and Marie never confused it with love or devotion. The men she dated, on the other hand, wanted to possess her; possessing her body for a night wasn't enough. Her Aunt Evangeline, the one person who understood her, warned her: *Most men are dull, they will need your spark to warm their beds and invigorate their lives but be wary, if they do not possess a similar light, they will resent it soon enough.* She wondered if Braun was different.

On her second day at the museum, Braun invited her to lunch. They sat outside under a Wild Pear Tree on a blanket he had tucked under his arm. His manner was calm yet formal. Marie guessed he came from an upper-class family the way he moved, so effortlessly with impeccable manners. Their conversation was sparce, but easy. He did not needle her about her past, why she wanted to work on the Broadwood, or her training. Instead, they talked about music. Exchanging thoughts on their most favorite pieces, the tricky brilliance of Beethoven's Opus 132, and other composers whose work inspired them most. Since that day, Marie hoped he would invite her out again. She was surprised he chose this as a second date, but she'd had brief affairs before, in fact, she only had brief affairs.

His familiar voice, the smell of his freshly pressed clothes, and his large hands which she saw as he circled her waist, a bold, sexy move. She did not want to run; she wanted this man even if it ended up being a one-time thing, something she was very used to. Gently, he turned her body toward him, softly kissing her at first and then pressing her body as close as he could, he kissed her with passion and urgency. She allowed him to lead her to the floor underneath the piano. The room was dark except for the soft glow coming from security lights which dotted the perimeter of the room. They made love under the piano, and Marie felt more alive than she had in years.

Afterwards, he held her close, something she did not expect. As Marie dosed off, he kissed her once more and left the room. Marie lay underneath the piano as it soothed her, whispering how beautiful she is, how desirable, and that she was chosen to be with them. Marie was only half listening; she was completely fulfilled and didn't care about the odd circumstance that led her here.

When she awoke, reality set in; she was naked and cold under the piano. It dawned on her someone might try to come in. She dressed quickly, turned on the lights, and inspected the piano. *No worse for the wear*, she thought. As she touched the piano, it sent a warm shiver throughout her body. For other people, what just happened would be outrageous, in fact, most people would not have let it happen, but for Marie, it was exciting. She knew herself well, she had an appetite for risk, but knew her limits. Even if this affair went no further than this one tryst, she could live with it.

Let me tell you about my Therese, Marie. I was in love with her. Oh, not the jealous love that humans bear but the admirable love my Master bore her and because of that, I loved her. She was a muse, our muse, inhabited by the most wanton, sweet spirit. She would play alongside him, the two of them commanding my keys together! I wanted her as he did, but I got plenty of her through him. For you see, I am greedy, and I would stay awake and alert in those hours before dawn or in the broad light of day when she would come to him, and he in a state of panic as he often was. Her voice was soothing not piercing streetcar bells like most of her time. She would sit by him on my bench, touch me first, loving me, stroking my keys with her gentle and intentional fingers so soft and pale. She would lean into me so that her breasts touched my keys and my wood,

34

and she would moan the softest, almost inaudible moan meant only for me.

In those days, I was alive more alive than if I was standing beside her made of flesh and blood, not wood and ivory. She breathed life into me, and as she was overcome with pleasure, I could feel her insides pulsing and rising as she whispered in ecstasy, please, please, ever so pleading ever so longing, I was her servant and she knew it.

The Master would hold her. His hands, those talented, magnificent hands created a symphony of orgasm inside her. She would beg him to make love to her, and he would oblige, pulling her down to the fine silk Naeem carpet below me. A foot leaning against my pedals kept the time and rhythm until they were both spent, and he could perform no more. In those moments, I was a beautiful wall shielding them from the entire world, protecting them and at the same time, enjoying them. My body, made of wood and wire strings, would tighten and release with their pleasure. I sweated and yielded to the master as did she, and I alone bear the responsibility of keeping the secret of their love, our love, the master, Therese Marie, and I.

How I tremble at these memories. They flow through me now like water in the Sahara, trickling along the dried-out sand of my heart where water pools and recedes, never filling the void. There can be no revival for me.

Do you want to know a secret? This young Marie was destined to find me. I am her teacher, and she is our pupil. She will help me release the secrets I've yet to tell because only into the hands of the fated one, must they fall. We've waited many years for her, but so too, have the bastards that want to harm her. Damn them!

Beethoven does not rest and so I do not rest. The letters have been stolen; Marie's life is in danger. If I cannot make her trust me, we are lost, all is lost.

Chapter Three

Sunday morning in Marie's temporary home, the Tordas winery, the guests are brunching together in the great room. The stone building is over one-hundred years old and was meticulously renovated keeping some of the most interesting aspects of its architecture. It offers the perfect respite from the bustle of Budapest. Marie is grateful the agent insisted she take a room here for her stay instead of in the city. Marie is famished, but is sheepish about last night with Braun; what if someone saw her come in so late? Like a schoolgirl who gets caught with her blouse buttoned wrong, Marie blushed as her body tingled from the memory. *What the hell, I'm forty years old, for Gods' sake.* She got dressed and headed downstairs.

The room, with its soaring wood ceiling and original stone fireplace, is filled with chatter as the guests eat and drink wine. Marie joins them and they welcome her, saying good morning in unison. She sits next to Viktor the older gentleman from Vienna who, in the morning light, looks much younger than she had originally thought. His eyes are bright, and his face handsome. He asks her about her work, and mentions he had a cousin who worked at the museum, and that they were both students of classical music.

"I play the violin, not very well, but it gives me great pleasure."

"What do you like to play?"

Viktor's eyes mist as he says, "Ah, sad songs, all about love, loss, and passion. What is life without passion?"

"Yes, indeed."

"My violin knows me, it knows when I need to play a love song or when my heart is aching, and I need to cry out with sadness. I think it speaks to me. Is that so strange?"

Marie hesitated. His violin speaks to him, this is a random coincidence, and yet, something inside told her there are no coincidences in Budapest.

"I would like to hear you play sometime."

"You shall, you shall. These walls are not so thick. If you hear me playing, come in anytime."

He touched her hand as he left. Marie sat a while longer, finishing her wine listening to the chatter around her. To be amongst people, but not having to talk is refreshing. She heard music, the unmistakable sound of the violin then Tilda's voice, like rattling gravel.

"Viktor, he's playing that ballad again, dragging his bow across those poor strings."

Her gruff assessment couldn't be further from the truth. Viktor's playing is melodic and woeful, you could hear a pin drop in the room. Someone started humming softly, the young couple got up to dance, swaying slowly, staring into each other's eyes. Even Tilda, with her chin in her hand, closed her eyes and drifted off in a waking daydream.

Marie's attention is drawn to the young couple dancing. A sense of sorrow surrounds them, they are tragic somehow, as if they are caught in a storm with nothing to hold onto, but each other. The young man, tall and skinny, his blonde hair falling over his eyes, his tattered shirt tucked neatly into his pants, tell the story of lack and maybe, of hope. He holds the young woman tightly, as she folds into him as if they are one person. Marie's heart is breaking for them without knowing why, her eyes mist.

The song ends and Marie waves them over to an empty spot at the table beside her.

"Hello, I'm Marie. You two dance beautifuly together."

"Thank you. My wife, Sarah, was a ballet dancer, I try not to stomp on her toes."

They both make a forced laugh in unison.

"I'm from America, I danced with the Huston City Ballet Company, until I met Hans. His family is here, we thought we would have a better life here in Budapest."

Sarah lowers her eyes as she finishes her sentence, Hans reaches for her hand.

Marie had to know, "Are you unhappy here in Hungary?"

Silence.

"We are not unhappy after all we are together; but we are broke. I cannot find work and my family is tired of helping us. I thought I would work in the family's business, but my brother, well he does not approve, and he runs the place now. It is not a good situation. My father owns a share in the winery, we stay here rent free, for now."

"I'm so sorry. Are you thinking of returning to America then?"

"We would like to. If we can save enough money, we would go back and live in Texas, near my family. But it's been hard."

"Hans, what kind of work are you looking for? I am on a temporary assignment in the Hungarian National Museum, maybe, I could talk to the director, see if there are any openings?"

"Oh Miss Marie, that would be wonderful! But I do not want to impose."

"Not at all, I'm happy to help."

They hear Viktor playing his violin again, Hans and Sarah say goodbye, and Marie walks toward the sound. She found Viktor in the courtyard just across from his room. He saw her and nodded, but kept playing. She settled herself on a stone bench and closed her eyes. She lost herself in the melody, so melancholy and sweet. When Marie opened her eyes, Viktor was seated next to her.

"Forgive me for intruding; I, too, love the sound of the birds softly trilling in the trees. It reminds me of hope."

"Hope, what an interesting thought, Viktor."

"Hope is something we cherish in Budapest, dear Marie. Hope for our children, hope for our art. I have something for you."

Viktor handed her a note and left her alone in the courtyard.

Marie opened the note:

More will be revealed. Meet me, now.

2203, Birch Street

Marie's first thought was to ask Viktor who gave him the note. Instead, she stayed put on the bench, her instincts sending shivers up her spine.

Go, learn!

The voice again. Marie silently acknowledged the piano and took a deep breath. She hoped the note was from Braun and decided it was worth an afternoon to find out. She did not recognize the address, but she was almost certain it was not in the city.

It took over forty-five minutes to get to Birch Street. It was far outside the city as Marie suspected, the drive took her deeper into the countryside. The driver turned off the road onto a long, tree-lined gravel driveway leading to a small stone mansion with white shutters and blue flowers planted along the entrance. Just as Marie was about to knock, the butler opened the door. She started to speak, but he interrupted her, "Madame Marie, this way." He led her into a small drawing-room, pointed out the tea service on the sideboard, and told her to make herself comfortable. The room is warm, and the paintings and etchings hung on every wall are very old, as if the whole house was stuck in another time. The portrait over the mantel caught her attention; a woman in a long, black velvet dress, yards of black velvet draped around her naked body secured by a diamond and ruby brooch of a piano. Marie could not look away. The resemblance is unmistakable. She moved very close to the painting and the eyes of Evangeline stared back at her. Marie's eyes misted; she would give anything to see Evangeline again, especially, here in Budapest. *Who is she?* Marie wondered as a chill spread up her spine, like the feathered cracking of ice on a frozen lake.

She did not hear his footsteps, but felt his presence behind her. She did not turn around. His breath was on her neck. "Upstairs," he whispered into her ear. She waited for a beat or two then turned around, and of course, he was gone. Marie looked at the woman in the painting again, she did not want to leave the room. *Is it you, Evangeline?*

Marie climbed the carpeted grand staircase to the second floor. When she reached the top, she turned left walking the long hallway until she noticed the last door ajar, light from the fireplace illuminating the hall. She slowly entered. The door shut behind her, and she stopped. His hands were at her waist, and his body pressing against hers.

"Please don't run."

Marie waited. What if she turned around and it was not Braun, but some deranged eccentric who lured her here to hurt her? What if it was the man in the library who gave her the letters? She summoned her courage and slowly turned toward him.

"Braun."

He said nothing, but came very close and kissed her, she opened her mouth to him, and her heart pounded with desire. The sun was setting, and shadows from the fire danced like leaping black snakes. He undressed her slowly as he kissed her neck, her shoulders, her breasts, her stomach, and she collapsed into him. He picked her up and gently laid her on the huge four-poster bed covered in soft sheets and pillows. When they were spent, Marie laid her head on his chest, listening to the steady beat of his heart. They didn't speak for a long while. Finally, it was Braun who spoke first.

"There are secrets you are now part of. Will you keep them?"

"Secrets? Sounds interesting." Marie yawned, her eyes closing. "But why me?"

"Only you."

He kissed her eyes as she drifted off to sleep. When she awoke, he was gone. On his pillow sat a sprig of lavender and two more letters. Marie sat up and gently opened them.

June 3, 1818

Forgive me. I will learn in time to soften your fears and temper your heartache, but never forget, this "fragile woman" loves you, and will love you through whatever befalls you.

I yearn for you still.

Yours

And the reply:

June 4, 1818

I have always been a fool, but never more so than now, begging at your delicate feet to forgive me. The world may toss me to the wolves, but never again shall you bear witness to the wicked beast inside me.

My love, my hope, come back to me.

Marie carefully put the letters back in the envelopes as she heard someone coming down the hall. She pulled the covers up to her chin and heard a knock at the door.

"Yes."

"He would have you down for breakfast, madame."

She was shocked. He's still here? She hurriedly dressed and stowed the letters in her bag. She made her way downstairs and found Braun in the dining room.

"You're still here."

"I live here."

"Ah, yes, of course."

He went to her, kissed her, and pulled out her chair.

"Braun…"

Before Marie could finish her sentence, Braun interrupted her.

"I'd like you to move in here."

"What?"

"I've much to tell you, and it will be easier if you are here."

Marie looked at him in the morning light. His messy salt and pepper hair, his shirt unbuttoned, the slight hint of stubble on his chin, and his blue eyes warm and sad. She wondered why he always looked sad.

"Is everyone in Budapest so direct? Braun, I'd like to know more about what's going on, especially, before I move in, I mean, we hardly know each other. What about the letters you left on my pillow, I need to know more, and who is the woman in the painting in the drawing room?"

Braun did not answer. Marie watched him drink his coffee and slice his eggs.

How strange, Marie thought.

"There is much to share with you Marie and there are some things I would like to know as well. For example, I'd like to know you will be in my bed every night."

Marie said nothing. She watched him. Braun looked her straight in the eye when he said this. No hesitation, no explanation. *He is an awkward man, this is obvious. He's sexy yes, but really, way too forward, and they say Americans are too forward, it would be comical if he wasn't so serious.* Marie's not typically insecure; she knows she has a certain appeal to men, and she has learned to use it. But Braun has a way of rattling her normally grounded mindset. He moves fast, that's not entirely a turn off, but it is surprising. At forty years old, Marie's peach skin still glows on her delicate face that is undeniably pretty. Her soft, blue eyes are the palest of blue giving her presence an ethereal quality, and her long, wavy dark brown hair shines almost black in candlelight with a crazy riot of dark red and chocolate in the sun. She is not tall, but because she is so lithe and thin, she looks taller than her five feet six-inch stature. Marie believed she would ever marry, and the thought did not alarm her. It would take a unique man to satisfy her need for intelligent conversation, her drive for sex, and mostly, her need for independence— a combination every man she met, found intolerable. She thought Braun was different, but right now, she can't bring herself to trust him, it's all moving too fast.

Fool, I know but trust him.

She heard the voice again.

"I can have your things moved for you if you like."

The hair on the back of her neck stood up, and her nerve endings were on fire. He went too far. Even if she would consider seeing him again after this awkward morning, asking her to move in is crossing the line. Who does he think he is? They spent one night together for God's sake. Marie's defenses are up and yet, a part of her wants to say yes, but she'd have to let her fears go, to forget her past disappointments with men. Doing this would be a huge stretch. Her gut told her to trust him, her heart was leaping from her chest, but still, she restrained herself. Old habits die hard for Marie, and she needed more time, more proof. How could she be falling for him so quickly? She reminded herself she is far away from home, jumping into an affair here would be risky, not to mention he is the director of the museum that hired her, she works for him.

Trust is a slippery ideal for Marie and she has a strong need to keep her independence. At times like this, Marie snaps into her default mode of shutting down if she feels pushed and Braun is certainly pushing her, *damn it!* His arrogance at not answering her direct question about the woman in the painting, the caviler way he asked her to move in, is unnerving. As Marie got up from the table and headed for the door, he touched her hand.

"I won't ever hurt you."

Marie moved her hand away from his, got into the waiting car from the museum, and told the driver to take off.

Chapter Four

Yes, Braun is my malleable pawn, I need him and yet how I loathe him! What a masterful player he is loving our Marie in my very presence. She is mine! Take an axe to me once, and for all you merciless Gods for even one who is dead, old wood, wire, and ivory can only sustain so much. I must make sure Braun does more than take his pleasure with her body. I am unholy, I am greedy and jealous, I want her for my own. If only I could take her into my strings, make her one with my frame, she would be mine forever, I would hunger no more. Or give me one night alive as any mortal man and she will yearn for him no more.

Braun József Illes is not an emotional man, he loves deeply, and above all the things he deems worthy of his love, music is a constant. His grandmother was one of the first famous female film composers, and his father was a concert pianist.

From an early age, Braun did not have to be coaxed into practicing the piano. He loved everything about the instrument and even did scale drawings of a piano he designed. His father's family helped fund the Hungarian National Museum centuries ago, and because Braun was a noted music historian, it was a given he would be caretaker of the archive of historical musical instruments. His family name is all over the museum, and he considered it his legacy to take care of this precious part of Budapest's history. He is also an accomplished pianist. He plays with a masculine forcefulness, not the lithe touch of Asian pianists or the cumbersome way of some Americans. His touch is masterful, purposeful, and poetic. Not unlike Beethoven himself. The piano ignited a desire in him and fueled his passion for life. He never married, but he has had his share of women.

Braun is picky. Obvious, big-busted women who rub against his arm at cocktail parties, bore him to tears. Women whose make up stains his sheets irk him beyond measure. He craves intelligence, curiosity, creativity, independence, and quiet beauty. Braun also needs someone who can keep up with his ravenous need for sex. At fifty, his sex drive is still formidable, and when he meets a woman who captivates him with her wit and intelligence and especially an appreciation for music, he isn't shy about bedding her. Braun's chiseled features, pale-blue eyes, and stoic six-foot three frame, get him noticed and feared. He learned at an early age to use his physical presence to his advantage.

He wants Marie, but more than that, he needs her. She possesses all the qualities he finds irresistible in a woman. But in her case, she is also part of a web of history that he himself is caught in. They would be tied together regardless of whether he was wildly attracted to her or not. This fact made things more complicated, but Braun never shied away from a challenge. And Marie represented a challenge he happily, greedily accepted.

Back at the winery, sitting on the bed, Marie can breathe once more. Why did she run? She did so on instinct, on autopilot. Marie never met a man she wanted to be with on a regular basis. When a man got too possessive, which is what she sensed in Braun, she ran. But with Braun, her heart is conflicted. She felt his possessiveness, but this time, it made her happy. She was not expecting that. *You're not a girl anymore, Marie, so what if you take a lover and let him make you happy? So, what it if doesn't last? You've been alone so long, is your solace really that wonderful? Who is the fool now!*

Marie berated herself for at least twenty minutes. When she finally tired of it, she began to laugh at herself. *He likes me, he is smart, handsome, and he knows about the letters. The letters!* She suddenly remembered he gave her two of the letters. He's connected to this. *Oh, Marie, what have you done!* At least she could have asked more questions before she left. Feeling childish and embarrassed, Marie hunted in her bag for her cell phone intent on calling Braun and explaining or trying to explain why she left. Three text messages were unread. She sat back on the bed and opened them. All from Braun, they read:

"I am an awkward man, I know, and I can be too direct, I'm sorry."

"Don't leave your work, I couldn't bear that."

"Just come back."

How could one man be so seductive, smart, and nice all at the same time? A rare breed this Braun. Marie wanted to go to him and yet, she sat on her bed not moving an inch. Giving in after taking a stand was not one of her strengths.

You must go!

She heard these words, clear as day as if someone was sitting right next to her. The soothing voice of the piano. "Why, why should I go?" She said back under her breath. Nothing. No voice, not a sound in the room except for her protective subconscious repeating the word *Ridiculous*. She picked up her phone and texted Braun:

"Dinner, out someplace?"

Within seconds came a reply:

"Yes. Meet me at Hampshire House. Eight p.m.?"

"Yes."

It suddenly dawned on her that she was tired, bone tired. Marie got very little sleep in Braun's bed. The thought of it made her body stir. It was the most romantic night she had had in a long time. He was a great lover yes, but more than that, he was so present. Braun is different from any man she has ever known, and Marie is drawn to him with a force she cannot ignore. But she can't lose herself completely. After all, she hardly knows him and yet, it feels like she's known him all her life. She was eager to know the history of the letters and where he got them. Should she tell him about the letters she had? The answer would have to wait. Marie fell back on the bed, adjusted the pillow, and fell fast asleep.

Marie woke just in time to shower and dress. She pawed through her closet, surveying her meger options. She decided on a plain, black crepe dress that skimmed her small frame nicely. She pinned up her hair in a sort of up-down style and wrapped her soft purple wool shawl around her shoulders. She almost made it to the front door when Tilda stopped her.

"Marie! I haven't seen you for days and now you are leaving again, a date, yes?"

This is tricky. How would she explain her date was with Braun? Just last week, she listened to Tilda go on and on about Braun and his "royal" family, what a greedy man he is, and she warned to Marie to stay away from him. At the time, Marie didn't care one way or the other about Braun. Now, she wouldn't hesitate to defend him. Tilda isn't someone to tangle with; Marie's instinct told her to back off.

"Umm, not a date, a group dinner to celebrate the restoration, goodnight."

She hurried out the door and ran into the waiting limo. On the way to the restaurant, she smiled to herself. *I don't care what anyone thinks. If I feel this good, it must be right.*

The restaurant is in a lovely, restored mansion, and as she walked in, Marie felt alive, a desirable woman having an incredible affair. A new air of confidence deep inside makes her smile. Braun walks up to Marie holding his hands out, staring straight into her eyes. The smell of his cologne, his strong hands, her body shivered in remembrance of his touch and his impossibly gentle eyes. Braun did not let go, he held Marie close.

"I can't tell you how happy you've made me. I am boorish at times, I know. I don't deserve a second chance, but I will never make you want to run away from me again, I promise."

Marie blushed and said, "I'll hold you to that."

Marie kissed Braun and he held her for few minutes more. She could not ignore the pounding of her heart or the way she felt at home in Braun's arms. She composed herself as she settled in her chair by not looking at him for a few moments. She made a process out of placing her purse at her side, straightening her dress, folding her shawl, and smoothing her hair. When she looked up, he was staring at her.

"Braun, you have to stop doing that."

"Never."

She smiled at him, and he returned it with a warm smile of his own.

"Wine?"

As he poured merlot in her glass, she melted into the moment, totally at ease, thinking there was no place on this earth she would rather be right now.

Their conversation was light, as Braun shared his family history and his fanatical love of music, especially Beethoven.

"Braun, I must hear you play the Broadwood."

"You shall. Is it ready?

"Not fully, but you could still play a bit for me, for purposes of my work, of course. It helps to hear what needs to be tweaked when someone else is playing."

"Of course. Perhaps you will let me play for you at my house. I have a Bösendorfer, not the Broadwood but, still a beautiful instrument.

"I would love that."

Marie excused herself for the powder room and when she returned, Braun was holding her purse and shawl and gently took her arm to leave.

"My car is just outside."

Marie let him lead her. Her insides simmering, and she could not snap herself out of the dream like state she is in. She's walking on air, every cell in her body is humming anticipating the feel of him inside her and his lips on her body. She would have gone anywhere and done anything with him in this moment. Once they were inside his car, he turned on the below dash light which gave off a soft purple glow. She could not remember if she pulled him toward her or if he pulled her to him, but time melted away as they kissed.

On the way to his house, he drove with one hand on the wheel and the other entwined in hers. She studied him. Fiercely handsome and sexy behind the wheel of his Ferrari, his legs so long his muscular thighs touched the steering wheel. But his face was soft and not stern, and the sweetness and simplicity of him reaching for her hand touched her heart.

In past relationships, this was precisely the moment Marie felt the walls closing in on her, and she'd be hatching her exit strategy. But tonight, Marie thought of nothing, but how at peace and happy she felt. She is not thinking of running, quite the opposite.

Inside Braun's house, they sip whiskey in the living room.

Marie walks over to the shiny, black Bösendorfer grand piano.

"Play for me?"

Braun sat at the piano bench and motioned for her to sit next to him. Instead, Marie pushed an overstuffed chair near him and said, "I want to hear *and* watch." She tossed off her shoes, crossed her legs, and motioned for him to start.

Braun settled himself then began to play. The melody is rich and woeful. He plays purposefully, but brilliantly. He let the finish of the melancholy notes linger just long enough like a dancer on point emerging from a pirouette. Marie did not recognize the piece, but it pulled at her, and tears began to well in her eyes. The movement of his body, the swaying of his shoulders, his eyes closing now and then; this was Braun speaking to her on a soul level. She knew him, she felt close to him as no other had been before. He was telling her the story of his heart, of the longing for a companion to know the truth of his needs, his dreams, and his desires. The dark places he sealed off from the world and the deep love he kept hidden for so long. Before he finished playing, Marie decided she would never leave him, not unless he forced her to. She had found her place to stay, her reason for staying, and quite possibly the love of her life.

He wiped his brow and took in a long breath. When he looked at Marie, she was softly weeping.

"Tears of joy, I hope."

She couldn't speak. She wanted to tell him what a gifted pianist he is, how effortlessly he becomes one with the instrument as so few do, and that she heard his story and felt his heart. She wanted to tell him she loved him, but those words were too far back in her throat to say.

"My beautiful Braun" was all she could manage to get out. He took her hand and held her.

"Come to bed, it's been a long day."

Quietly they undressed and nestled in close together under the soft down blanket. He sensed her thoughts were still far away. With her head resting on his chest, they drifted off to sleep in matter of minutes.

Like our Therese Marie, just like Beethoven, she allows music to make her weep, to feel every human emotion without regret. It makes me yearn for her even more. Her mother, Therese Marie, was a singular woman deeply in love with Beethoven. Most women in Beethoven's life wanted to be near him for the notoriety of it but cared nothing for his tender heart. He had such prose in his soul and how he anguished over powdered breasts that tilted in their corsets only to tease and court but never allowing him to touch.

Sitting by his side at my keys, listening, and making him laugh, Therese Marie's heart skipped beats as he played. I could feel the uneven pounding of it as she leaned into him. She was his muse, his lifeline, and he hers. I would glow and warm when they made love in the same room or underneath my virile frame. Theirs was a rhythm that comforted me, how I longed to embrace them both, and protect them. Alas, I am only wood, ivory, and wire. I am an inanimate object, not human. But still, I yearned for her touch, too. Young Marie deserves the same kind of love even if it is with that fool Braun, I must acquiesce. For only those who can feel extraordinary love would understand what is at stake. Beethoven's one sacred true love. Marie will surely protect them.

Chapter Five

The next morning Marie's phone was chirping with text messages, one after the other non-stop. Braun leaned over her to pick it up.

"Meine Liebe, someone really needs to talk to you."

Marie stared at him. Meine Liebe, that's what he called her. Just like Evangeline. Her mind seized for a moment.

"Marie, are you OK? Do you want me to answer it?"

"No, no, I'm sorry."

She kissed Braun and looked at her phone. It was Tilda.

"Someone has broken into my room at the winery."

"What? How can that be."

Well, to be honest it's not the first time. Someone broke in the third day I was here. Nothing was missing they just made a mess of the place."

"Marie, we should talk about the letters. Let's get dressed."

Marie watched Braun grab his clothes and head into the bathroom. She texted Tilda a short note to say she would be home soon and got out of bed. They piled their plates with fresh croissants, cheese, and fruit and headed to the living room to sit by the fire. Braun looked serious and stressed. She reached for his hand.

"What is it?"

"The letters I gave you, you said someone gave you others, yes?"

"Yes, I was in the Palace library, and someone handed them to me in an old book but then disappeared. Do you know where these letters are coming from?"

"Yes, I think I do. Marie, it might sound strange, but I think you were meant to be in Budapest just now. Did your aunt Evangeline tell you anything about your ancestors?"

"No, not really why?"

Braun dropped his head and stared at the fire. Marie sensed whatever he said next would be hard for her to hear. She braced herself.

"Meine Liebe, I know I should not be the one to tell you this, but here we are. Forgive me for being direct, it's how I am. I believe you are a direct descendant of Beethoven, perhaps the last of the pure line."

Marie remained quiet. She wasn't sure if Braun was crazy or if she was.

"Braun it can't be. How do you know this?"

"I hesitate to tell you things your family should have told you. I am falling in love with you, and I don't want you to run or think that I am part of this plot."

Stunned, Marie replayed what he just said in her head: He is in love with her and there is some kind of plot. If ever there was a good time to run, it would be now, but she did that once already and ended up right back here. No, she would stay and try to figure out what this is all about.

"Braun, I don't know what to say. I feel so close to you, I feel…"

"No need to return the sentiment, Meine Liebe. I know I have overwhelmed you. All you need to know is that I will be with you throughout this. You can trust me, always."

Marie wanted to acknowledge that Braun admitted his love her and she longed to do the same. But, a sense of urgency filled her body and she decided their talk of love would hold; she needed to know about her connection to Beethoven.

"But, Beethoven? Can you tell me more, maybe, start from the beginning?"

"Your Aunt Evangeline, she… she was not your aunt she was your biological mother. She and her third cousin had a relationship, but did not marry. When she became pregnant with you, he married the woman you know as your mother. They did this so Evangeline and he could be close to you. They are both direct descendants of Beethoven's, but you are the last child. You are the last living direct descendant."

The mention of Evangeline's name startled Marie. It was like two worlds colliding, her life in America and her life now in Budapest. Marie hadn't told Braun very much about her aunt that she could recall; she searched her memory of the scant few times she and Braun have been together and if she mentioned Evangeline's name, it could not have been more than once. This conversation is getting very curious and little scary. *Who is Braun, how does he know so much about Evangeline and her family, especially intimate details Marie didn't even know!*

"Wait, wait a minute. First off, my father and I were not that close. If he wanted me with him, he never showed it. Both my parents left me sometimes for months at a time with Evangeline."

"I do not know all the details, but I do know Evangeline loved you so. She wanted you to come to Budapest, she also wanted to protect you from this secret and the secret of the letters."

Marie was on her feet and when Braun came near, she put up her hand to single for him to keep his distance. Deep in thought, she wasn't sure which question to ask next. For example, why didn't he just come clean with her the moment she walked into the museum? Did he make love to her as way of manipulating her into trusting him? After all he has claimed to know some very personal things about her. If he's trying to get close to her for some other reason than he cares for her, she will make sure he regrets it.

Marie let her instinct to be wary of trusting him, take over. She needed to know for sure what his intentions were and she needed to know, now.

"I find it very convenient you don't know all the details, just enough to try and unnerve me. Braun, I need you to start at the beginning. Right now, I don't trust you and you've put me in a very vulnerable position, which I'm guessing was your plan all along. If you are trying to manipulate me, you will find I am not such an easy mark. I have no idea how you know these things about my family, providing it's true, or if it's something you made up for some gain you think you will achieve. But Braun, hear me plain, I will not be played with. You will regret ever meeting me if this is some kind of sick game you're playing at. I may be far from home, but I am not a child, I know how to take care of myself."

"Marie, please, I know this is a lot to digest, but I am telling you the truth. I've no wish to hurt you or manipulate you, in fact, it's quite the opposite. If you will sit and give me the chance to fully explain, you might better understand. If you still don't trust me, you are free to leave anytime, I would never keep you here against your will. I give you my word on that."

Marie sat in the chair by the fireplace, across from the small sofa where she motioned for Braun to sit. She wanted to keep some space between them. The physical attraction between them is true enough, but if he turned out to be some kind of manipulative nut case, Marie wanted to see it clearly in his eyes from across the room, not from lying in his arms.

"OK, I will give you fifteen minutes. Talk."

"Thank you. I will start with the story of Beethoven, some things, I don't think you know. He did not die childless or unmarried. His secret lover, as you know, is known to the world only as the Immortal Beloved; but she was not anyone the history books suspect she was. We still don't know her name, but she was pregnant with his child when he died. They had a pact to keep her identity and their relationship secret and of course, the secret of their child."

"How is it you know this, and I don't or maybe, a better question is, why don't any of the noted music historians know?"

Braun remained silent for a moment. Maire shifted in her chair, letting out a long sigh.

"I can't answer as to why historians do not know, but I can tell you how I know. My great grandfather was well connected in Budapest. We cannot be sure, but we think he knew the Immortal Beloved. Of course, he knew Beethoven as well as most of the wealthy families in Budapest did, so we surmise her knew who Beethoven's secret lover was. My great grandfather was a horrid man and to be honest, so was my grandfather and my father. We think this portrait of the woman in black velvet is the Immortal Beloved, but again, we are not sure. My father told me the painting must never leave the family. He never said why. It was a direct order he gave me and my brothers. My father knew Evangeline. I do not know the extent of their relationship, but he did know her. He knew who she was, he knew she was Beethoven's descendant. He told me the story of her affair with her cousin and that she was pregnant. If we asked him any direct questions regarding Beethoven, the Immortal Beloved, or Evangeline, he would not answer them. But he did tell me about the letters. Apparently, the letters are the source of knowledge, they are how we know that Beethoven and his secret lover married and had a child. That's everything I know."

Marie's mind is clicking away like a well-oiled gear. She memorized everything Braun said and had questions, pointed questions.

"Why would you assume your great grandfather knew Beethoven or his secret lover?"

"Because he was a silent partner in funding Beethoven's concerts, as well as his patron, paying for his rooms, his doctors, even for the Broadwood."

"Oh my God, that certainly is not documented in any of the history books."

"No, it is not. I suspect it's because the funding came with an awful lot of blackmail."

"Blackmail? Braun, this story gets more fantastic by the minute. I want to know more about that, but right now, I want to know how your father met Evangeline?"

"That, I do not know. I do know he was, how do you say, obsessed with her to some degree. My father kept a diary for a few years, he believed someone would write his life story someday. In it, he talks about meeting her at a ball and how he wanted to possess her. There was not a lot of detail, but it is written in his diary, by his own hand."

"All right, now for the most important question. If you knew all this about me before I set foot in Budapest, why did you wait until now to tell me? Why didn't you give me the letters first thing and explain all this the first day I came to the museum?"

"I don't have a good reason. In truth, by telling you, I am betraying my father's wishes. I did not expect to… like you or love you. I did not expect to feel anything for you. I was resigned to let you do your job and leave Budapest without ever mentioning the letters or anything about the Immortal Beloved. But the letters started turning up and I knew trouble was heading your way. When you told me someone pushed the letters into your hands in the library and that your room was ransacked, I knew I had to tell you what I knew. I would have told you anyway because I am falling in love with you, as I have admitted. But now, with all that has happened, I want nothing more than to make sure you are safe."

"Braun, I won't deny I am overwhelmed, you overwhelm me. Your honesty is hard to discount. Not many men would so readily admit they are in love and yet, you do so without hesitation."

"I'm not like other men, this I know. I am an awkward musician, a social misfit, and believe it or not, I have never fallen in love before. I've had women, yes, but I've never cared for anyone as I care for you."

Marie's eyes misted; her heart is breaking. She can't admit it to Braun, but she is falling for him too, but there's just too much in the way of their happiness now. Most of all, she has to be sure he's telling her truth.

"Braun, I don't want to seem ungrateful to you, because I am truly grateful for your kindness and your honesty, especially now. But I have to ask, and I hope you understand. May I see your father's diary?"

Without hesitation, Braun got up from the sofa and said, "Of course."

Marie waited by the fire, staring at the flames, the pop and crackle of the wood the only sound in the room. She needed Braun now, she hoped they could get past this.

"You can take your time, read it now or read it later, I trust you Marie and I understand why you need to see it."

Marie held the diary in her lap. She thought about leaving, sitting on her bed in the B&B and reading it alone. She heard the piano.

Read and trust him, you must!

Marie opened the diary. She thumbed through the pages as Braun sat on the sofa watching her. She found an entry that made her stop:

May 1976

She kept her appointment, much to my surprise and delight. She challenged me, but her kiss gave her away, she wants me, she cannot deny it. She thinks being bold would scare me away, how wrong she is. She is exquisite even when she is lying. I'll give her what she wants, it costs me nothing, but she will be mine. Her body, every inch will be mine. My sweet Evangeline, you know not what awaits you.

Tears are falling from Marie's eyes. She closes the diary and hands it to Braun. He gingerly kneels at her side by the chair.

"Please let me take you in my arms, I want nothing more than to comfort you."

Marie stands and allows Braun to hold her. They stand in front of the fire for a long moment.

"I'm OK, it's just going to take a bit of time for me to process this. But your father's diary is clear. It's incredible to think of it."

"It is Meine Liebe, but I am here, I'm not leaving your side unless you force me to."

Marie laughs a nervous attempt to lighten the mood.

"I'm not sure which fantastic thing to stew over, the fact that I am Beethoven's descendant or the fact that Evangeline was my real mother. It all makes sense now why my parents left me with Evangeline so often and why my mother was so cold and distant toward me. But why, why didn't Evangeline tell me?"

"We cannot know what was in her heart, but perhaps, she thought she had more time."

"More time, I wish we did have more time. It's one thing not to tell me she was my real mother and quite another thing to hide the fact that we are Beethoven's descendants, I mean, it's like something from a movie script."

"And yet, it's true. I cannot speak for Evangeline or Beethoven, obviously, but perhaps it follows the arc of his story. He wanted his love for her to remain a secret, he wanted to protect the one person in his life he truly loved, and who loved him. Not unlike what Evangeline did, yes?"

"Oh Braun, I just don't know. I am hurt Evangeline never told me. I loved her like she was my mother and yes, she loved me as well. It just feels like a betrayal somehow, but it that can't be right. Maybe, I'm being childish, I think I need to sit with this awhile."

"I don't think you are being childish; it seems natural. But please, remember, she loved you, she cared for you and showed you nothing, but love and kindness. If she was afraid to tell you the truth, perhaps it can be forgiven. After all, she was only human like the rest of us."

Marie fell into Braun's arms. She knew he was right; it was just all so shocking. Not the worst news to hear, she had a loving mother, and her ancestor is one of the greatest composers of all time, and a musician she has always admired. It's just a lot to take in in one afternoon.

"Braun, you make a lot of sense. I'm sorry if I hurt you, I could not imagine the things you said were true. But I do believe you, thank you for caring enough about me to tell me, and above all, thank you for being my friend."

"I'll always be here for you, Meine Leibe."

Braun poured Marie a small glass of whiskey and she drank it in one sip.

"Thanks, that helps, another please. Braun, tell me more about the letters. Who found them and where have they been all these years?"

"It's another secret our families have kept for centuries. I think because of this, you and I were destined to meet."

Marie sat facing him crossed legged on the couch.

"I need to know, tell me everything."

"I am sure you know the history of the museum. My direct descendants started the Hungarian National Museum with a gift of a library in 1802. From there it grew with another collection, a mineral collection donated by my great, great grandfather. My family knew Franz Liszt and so when he died, he donated the Broadwood to the museum in 1874."

"I knew the provenance of the Broadwood, but I did not research your family. So, what's the secret?"

"After the piano was donated by Liszt's estate, it sat in a sealed room for years. It was scheduled to be restored and then played for a short concert to raise money for the museum. A well-known technician at the time was hired. No one bothered him and no one oversaw his work. If it wasn't for a custodian with a heart of gold and a love of classical music, we would never have found out about the letters."

Chapter Six
Zoltan Cherneskvy, 1889

Irinna Cherneskvy was wrapping hardboiled eggs in a soft cloth along with some cheese and a large chunk of bread for his lunch as she did every day. Zoltan was lucky. Most of the people in the village did not have his work, an admirable job at the Hungarian National Museum. He cleaned floors and dusted, but he was trusted with some of the world's most precious and timeless treasures, none more precious than Beethoven's 1817 Broadwood fortepiano. Zoltan relished Beethoven's music and dreamt at night by the fire that he was a pianist. As he closed his eyes, he smelled the wood of the piano, felt the coldness of the keys, and was swept up in the music which fed his heart. His hands would sweep the air as he played his imaginary piano in the finest opera houses. A sober man with the soul of an artist, Zoltan took his responsibility very seriously. He lovingly polished the Broadwood and talked to it like a friend. He swore some days it spoke back to him.

"How is the master today. They tell me you will be restored again and played by some other fool to celebrate Beethoven. He should do you justice I would think, but if he does not, feel free to smack his hands with your lid."

All fools!

"Ah yes, they are. I will be here watching. You know Zoltan will watch with the eyes of a hawk. Care not my count, I will watch."

One chilly February morning the museum director introduced Zoltan to Leopold Truss, the famous piano technician who would restore the great Broadwood. Zoltan shook his hand with formality and a bit of malice. He grasped it firmly at first as was customary but, then squeezed it just a bit too hard and stared straight into the man's eyes.

"It is your honor to work the greatest piano of all time. Treat him well."

The man winced, wrangled his hand free, and stepped away from Zoltan who was standing only inches from his eyes.

"I will commence with my work, I will not disturb you, should you require anything, I am pleased to serve you."

Zoltan walked away and began adjusting the curtains on the back wall. Leopold never noticed Zoltan watching him even when his back seemed to be turned. Leopold opened his case and placed his instruments contained in a neat roll of velvet tied with a leather string, next to him. Each instrument of polished brass and steel was secured in its own velvet pocket. He looked in the direction of Zoltan who appeared to be busy brushing invisible crumbs off the carpet under the giant window.

Leopold took off his coat and went straight to the piano, bent down, and laid under it. He took off a panel of wood carefully, and painstakingly. It seemed to Zoltan that he was pretending to do something; but the man knows exactly what he was doing. He laid the piece near him on a carpet began to take out another panel. This time he hesitated before he gently laid the panel beside him. He flashed a look in Zoltan's direction and with a swift, deft movement, he lifted a small package out and slid it inside his satchel. He then laid the panel down and proceeded to get on with his work.

Alarm was rising in Zoltan. He saw the man remove the package from the undercarriage of the piano. He saw him slip it into his satchel. Zoltan wanted to run to him and beat him, take the package. But what could it be? Perhaps it was instructions that each technician leaves for the other. Maybe, he was alarmed for no good reason. The man seemed innocent enough and kept on working as before. Zoltan decided to wait and see if he could get a closer look.

"Help me!"

Zoltan heard the cry and took off in the direction of the man. Leopold looked out from underneath the piano completely nonplussed. His voice taught, clearly annoyed, he said, "May I help you?"

"I heard you ask me for help, no?"

"No, why would I need your help? You are mistaken." Leopold curtly dismissed Zoltan and went back to work.

Zoltan was confused, but he too, went back to the carpet and the drapes and did not press him. Soon it dawned on Zoltan that the voice came from the piano. He knew it was a crazy notion, but there could be no other reason. He had heard, or thought he heard the piano speak to him before. Now, perhaps, it was urging him to hear it.

The hair on the back of his neck was rising. Before he could talk himself out of it, he was on Leopold easily tossing him aside away from his satchel and instruments. He quickly reached into the satchel and pulled out the package. Leopold rushed him, but Zoltan deftly knocked him down again with one hand. He ordered him to stay still, or he would knock him unconscious. Leopold was dazed and bruised clutching his side he could not overtake Zoltan and he knew it. Zoltan pulled out the package and gently untied the twine rope. Letters, so many letters. At first Zoltan felt ashamed and was ready to hand them back to Leopold, but he caught a glimpse of a letter written in German and stopped. He recognized the entwined letters on the broken red wax seal and knew right away the incredible history he held in his hands. He wrapped them back up and slipped them into his apron pocket.

Zoltan pulled Leopold up off the floor and held him by his shirt collar close to his eyes.

"These are mine now. If you tell anyone, I will find you and you will regret it. Leave now while your legs are not broken and never return."

Leopold gathered his things with haste and left, but not before he gave a warning of his own.

"You think you can stop us, but you are wrong. Many others will come, the truth will be told!"

It was on that night so many years ago that Zoltan's life was changed forever. The next day he brought the letters to the museum and insisted on talking to the museum director alone. Joszef Franc Illes was a good man and treated the employees of the museum as family.

Although his entire staff consisted of only five people, he made sure their families had everything they needed, even if salaries alone did not cover it. Zoltan felt sure he could be trusted, and he was right. Zoltan and Józef formed a bond and a pact to protect the letters and keep them secret. They recruited others they were sure they could trust. In both families, there were trusted family members who would keep the secret of the letters safe for almost two hundred years.

Last May Zoltan's great grandson, Tamas, passed away at the early age of forty-three from brain cancer. Tamas was so like Zoltan. A melancholy boy, sensitive and creative he bonded with his grandfather, Zoltan Cherneskvy III, easily. His grandfather trusted Tamas to carry on the secret of the letters. He did not know how close to death he was. Tamas never married and he did not trust his brother or his sister enough to bring them into the secret of the letters. Instead, he found a loyal friend in his nurse who lived with him during the last two years of his life.

On a cold November night, wracked with pain and delusions, he made his nurse Henrik retrieve the letters from underneath the floorboards of his bedroom. Henrik was a good friend to Tamas and would never betray him. Unfortunately, Henrik's girlfriend Margarette, was a con artist and a thief who had no trouble stealing from anyone.

Margarette was also a beauty, but she had a nasty temper and was so good at lying she had trouble remembering what the truth was and what she had made up. She found thirteen of the secret letters and knew enough about classical music from Henrick to know they could be valuable. She began asking around for where she could sell them among her smarmy friends and finally, she found someone. Just as Beethoven's relatives created a secret cohort of those who would protect the letters, there was a secret cohort called, the Hungarian Historical Preservation Society, who worked to steal all eighteen of them and sell them to the highest bidder. By selling the letters, everyone in the cohort would benefit. A single letter at auction could fetch six figures. But the real monetary value of the letters was in the criminal case members of the (HHPS) could bring against the Illes family and the state. The Illes family, one of the oldest families in Budapest, also happens to be one of the wealthiest families in the world.

Braun finished recounting the story of the letters and poured himself a large whiskey. Marie could see he was anxious; his eyes misted over. Marie's head is spinning, but she needed to know more. If she was involved in this, she needed to know everything Braun knew.

"Braun, you said there were eighteen letters total, Margarette found thirteen, have the others been found?"

"I think only one remains lost. I gave you the two I had, the man in the bookstore gave you two, that makes seventeen letters total."

"But, why? If someone wants to make sure we get the letters, why don't they contact us, why play a shadow game?"

"Remember Leopold Truss? It seems he kept a diary. The thugs Margarette sold the letters to are greedy and figured out the diary, the story, and the letters all hold great value especially here in Budapest. He brought the letters to the consulate and charged my family with theft and conspiracy to steal national historic documents; a charge in Budapest that comes with jail time and could shut down the museum permanently. Anyone who holds the letters is considered an accomplice. Technically, we are breaking the law and now, you are, too."

"I could care less about that, but I am afraid for you and your family. Does the consulate still have the letters?

"A contact on the inside told us the letters have disappeared. The two I gave you were given to me months ago, sent by anonymous post. I have no idea who sent them. We can only hope the others were put in a safe place by members of our group. But we know nothing for sure.

We have lawyers working around the clock, but we could be jailed at any time, the museum could fall into the hands of scandals who would sell off everything and shut it down forever. Organized crime in Budapest has far reaching tentacles."

Marie did not respond right away. The room was silent except for the soft crackle of the fire. The air in the room seemed heavy, weighted down with all they had shared. So many thoughts and questions clouded Marie's mind. Still, running away was not one of them.

"Braun am I... a direct descendent of Josephine Brentano, she's the most likely candidate to be the Immortal Beloved, so they say. Do you think so?"

"From the history my family has told me, no, I do not think so. I believe there was another woman, unknown to anyone who was the real last love of Beethoven's life. She came into his life in the last few years of his, she was much younger. She was not connected to anyone he knew, none of the people documented in the historical accounts."

"But supposedly, the Immortal Beloved love letter was written while Beethoven was in Teplice. That means, some unknown woman, there at the same time, was his love and no one knew it? Even people in Teplice knew who Beethoven was, they would have been seen by someone. That doesn't add up."

"No, you are right. But to piece this together, we must forget everything we have read about Beethoven and his secret lover. Either historians missed the real clues, or they had nothing to go on. The history was written with the evidence they found. But that doesn't mean our Beethoven did not outsmart them. He knew he could not bring his lover out in the open. Most likely she was already married or so much younger than him, that her father would have had forced Beethoven to never see her again facing grave consequences to his livelihood, his music, if he did not comply. He would have been banned from performing, he would have been made more of an outcast than he already was. We simply don't know the truth, and, in my heart, I think that's exactly the way Beethoven wanted it."

What Braun said resonated deeply with Marie. In her heart, she felt the same. Beethoven's story is tragic, and, in his time, unforbidden love was insurmountable. Neither Beethoven or his secret lover would have been able to withstand the harsh treatment and banishment from society that surely would have happened. And to think she was pregnant with his child at time of his death, well, that's the most tragic part of all.

"I understand, I feel the same way you do. So, tell me, do you have a theory?"

"We believe he met her when he returned to Vienna. I know the infamous unsent letter to the Immortal Beloved was supposedly written in Teplice, but that is only one snapshot of the whole story. My father told us the other letters make it clear; this woman came into his life much later and their romance was unlike any other. But, the most important thing is, whoever the Immortal Beloved was, you are a direct descendant of hers so it is only right that you should decide what to do with the letters. I won't lie, you could become rich beyond your dreams if you were to turn the letters and his story over to the authorities."

"But why on earth would I do that, Risk you being jailed, and losing the museum? Braun, I would never do that. But maybe, you only want me because I can keep you out of jail."

Braun's face remained unchanged, and he stared straight into Marie's eyes, not saying a word.

Maire instantly regretted saying it. Only a short hour ago she confronted Braun and told him she did not trust him. That moment had passed, and he produced the proof she needed to believe him. She needed to make amends.

"No, I don't think really think that. Forgive me. I trust you Braun, completely."

They sat in silence for a long while. Braun staring into his glass of whiskey, Marie across from him staring into the fire. The old clock in the hall chimed seven o'clock and the butler came in and announced dinner. Neither one of them moved.

"Beethoven's Immortal Beloved could have been anyone," Marie said in low voice.

"Indeed."

Chapter Seven

This young Marie, she doesn't realize how special she is. Her heart is pure, her soul full of magic. How could she be anything but magical? She is the great Van Beethoven's last heir and the blood of the Immortal Beloved runs in her veins. I cannot leave this plane of time without knowing she is safe for she is mine, too.

Beethoven had many women; this you know, but why her? Why, when he was so much older and sicker could he have found love? But Beethoven was not like any other mortal man. He controlled the tides and commanded the moon. If you think I exaggerate, then you have not really listened to his music. Could a talent like his be merely mortal? Ah, but his legacy is not just music, it is love—a love he was never supposed to have had. In our time, he was thought a madman, a brute. So many fathers of tender young women from the finest families, shooed him away, slammed doors in his face; he was a brilliant tool of the God's but never was he allowed to have love. Therese Marie was like him in many ways. She cared nothing for the vain sentiments of the time, she loved him, madman or not.

I will protect our young Marie; I will make sure she finds the letters and returns them to the Immortal Beloved. Hurry Marie, they draw near!"

Agotha Farkas is just about to walk into Postesevk's, a posh women's dress shop in downtown Budapest, a place she has no business going to since her bank account is overdrawn, again. The red and silver cocktail dress is the most exquisite thing she has ever seen. She had to try it on and maybe, when she got her money, she would buy it. Her phone buzzed and she jumped.

"What?"

"Oh sorry, Yolsvky, I thought you were someone else. Yes, I will be there, six thirty with the girl. Viszontlatasra, goodbye."

Agotha took a deep breath. The last thing she needed to do was to piss off the head of the Hungarian Historical Preservation Society (HHPS). She shook off her momentary fear and proceeded to the Tordas winery to pick up Sarah. Tonight was important, and Sarah needed to prove she could be trusted. If it didn't go well, there could be consequences for her and for Sarah. Agotha was not about to let that happen.

She rang the doorbell to the winery and Tilda answered. She quickly ushered Agotha in as if she was expecting her. Viktor was reading a newspaper in the great room, listening to every word. He knew exactly who Agotha was, but couldn't blow his cover, not yet. He hoped Sarah was not as naive as she seemed and that she would catch onto Agotha's plan and realize she could not be trusted. He wanted to believe this, but looking at her now, with her fuzzy cream-colored sweater and happy red mittens, his heart sank.

They hurried out of the winery to Agotha's car, a rusted thing with a hole in the floorboards, it barely ran, but Agotha planned to get a new car just as soon as the story broke, and she got her money. Sarah shivered and asked her to turn on the heat.

"Sorry, cupcake, you will just have to freeze like the rest of us. The heat doesn't work in this thing, just button your coat."

Sarah winced at Agotha's words. Occasionally, it seemed Agotha was a different person from the fellow dancer and music lover she met in the library. She would be curt and harsh to Sarah and now she felt a mild sense of panic. She shoved the feeling back down her throat and kept quiet. As they neared the house where the meeting took place, Agotha spoke.

"I'm sorry my friend, I should not have snapped at you. I am so ashamed of my car and feel so bad about having to make you freeze out here in this cold. Please forgive me."

"No problem, Agotha, I understand."

"Good. Now, you must listen closely to me. These people are not, not, how you say, friendly. They are all business. They will test you to see if you really want to help or if you are a spy for the other side. You will have to watch what you say and say only few words. You understand this?"

Sarah's fear was rising like a volcano. She wanted to beg Agotha to take her back, something was wrong, it didn't feel OK anymore. She desperately wanted to leave.

"Agotha, maybe, I am not the right person for this. I'm not strong like you are, and I don't understand Hungarian or the ways of…"

"You will do this! I need you and they need you. If you back out now, you will be marked as a traitor, is that what you want?"

"Wait, what are you talking about? I am not a traitor I haven't done anything! Take me back, now!"

Agotha, had seen this kind of reaction before in people who thought they wanted to help, but in the end were weak. She despised Sarah right now and wanted nothing more than to slap her in the face and leave her on the street to freeze. But she took a deep breath and reminded herself that Sarah was her ticket to wealth and freedom. All the things she desperately wanted like that cocktail dress, a new car, a new life, fame, all hinged on getting Sarah to do as she was told. She had to change her approach if this was ever going to work.

"You're right. I am a horrible person. I am not so strong, and I am not very wise. All I know is that my country needs me to do this small thing to preserve the greatest piece of history we have. My own life does not matter, but yours does. I cannot ask you to do this, it's not your country. We would be rich beyond our dreams, but if I lose your friendship, I have nothing."

Agotha rummaged in her purse for the car keys, making a show of pretending to start the car again, hoping Sarah wouldn't take too long to change her mind.

"No, no, I'm sorry. You've been nothing, but a great friend to me, the only friend I have made since I have been here. Please forgive me. Let's put this behind us, I'm OK, let's go in."

Agotha murmured, *finally,* under her breath as they got out of the car.

The small house was filled with people and yet, it was eerily quiet. Sarah followed Agotha to the kitchen where three men sat at the table. They barely looked up when the girls walked in, but one of them, a large man in a blue wool hat motioned for them to sit. Agotha, pulled out a chair and pushed Sarah into it.

They stared at her, but no one spoke.

Finally, the man in the blue wool hat broke the silence.

"So, Agotha, you come here with this American girl. Does she know who we are?"

"Yes, I told her…"

"No, you shut up, let her speak for herself."

Sarah, cleared her throat and spoke, her voice shaky.

"I know you are members of a society, a society of people who want to return Beethoven's letters to the Hungarian government where they belong; so, everyone can know the true story of Beethoven."

"Yes, that's who we are, but you, you are an American, why are you here?"

"I—I, want to help."

"Why would you, an American girl want to help us?"

"I love classical music and I need money."

Silence. Agotha, who was standing behind Sarah, touched her shoulder and Sarah felt her cheeks flush red.

83

"Ah, yes, well, I need something too. Perhaps you and Agotha can give it to us. Agotha has given it to us before," the man said laughing as the others joined in.

"Istvan, don't scare her she is naïve. She is trustworthy, I vouch for her."

Sarah was frozen in fear. The men were talking in Hungarian laughing and pointing to her. She was sure that any minute now, she would be raped and beaten, and she would never see Hans again. Hans, her beautiful husband who had told her he had a change of heart. He did not want her to get caught up in this. He begged her not to go with Agotha and they fought before she left. She called him a coward. How stupid she was!

"No! No! I want to go back, take me back!"

Sarah jumped up from the table and threw herself on Agotha, beating her with her fists and screaming to take her back to the winery. Agotha tried not fall, but she could not withstand Sarah's fists and besides, Sarah was a good two feet taller than she. Agotha twisted her ankle and fell on the floor. In a moment the man in the wool cap was on Sarah, pulling her away from Agotha and yanking her head back by her hair, yelling at her in Hungarian. Sarah kicked and tried to escape, but one of the men had a knife and he waved in front of her face.

"I can shut you up with this or you can stop screaming right now!"

Agotha begged Sarah to stop screaming and to calm down, but she would not. Sarah was still thrashing when the man in the wool cap let go of her, pushing her toward the man with the knife whose head was turned yelling at

Agotha. He did not react quickly enough. The five-inch blade pierced Sarah's throat almost through to the back of her neck.

The room was silent as he pulled the knife out of her throat, and she fell with a thud onto the carpet. Immediately people began to scatter out of the house. Agotha, the man in the wool cap and the man with the knife stood in silence. Agotha, sensing that she might be in danger turned to run, but the man with the knife caught her by the hair.

"You go nowhere. Sit."

Agotha sat down and began to weep. The men spoke in Hungarian, picked up Sarah and dragged her body outside into a patch of frozen grass in the back of the house. When the men returned, the man with the knife sat in front of Agotha and wiped the blade clean with a dish towel.

"Now, you belong to us. In order to let you leave, you must make bargain for your life. No one knows the members of this group by name and now, we have a murder on our hands. Not our first mind you, but she's a foreigner, an American of all things. They will be looking for her and cause us much trouble. What are you going to do about it?"

Agotha struggled to form words. She spoke in her native tongue because she could hardly think.

"I will write to her husband; tell him she and I were having an affair and we left Budapest together."

"*Hmmm*, clever, but not sure it will be that easy. His family is Hungarian, no?"

"Yes."

"Then he will be here forever looking for her, looking for you. How will you hide from him and how can you ensure we will not be exposed?"

Agotha, had no answer. She put her head down and sobbed.

"I don't know, I, I will do whatever you say, but please, don't kill me. I have nothing, and I need to be part of this, please!"

"Pitiful girl you are. OK, write letter, but from now on, you live here."

Agotha could not argue she had nothing left inside. She wasn't so sure now if letting them kill her wouldn't be better than living with what had just happened. It was her fault and now, she would have to pay for it for the rest of her life. An older woman came in and gently lifted Agotha from the chair. Agotha looked at her with tears streaming down her cheeks.

"I take care of you now. Come."

Chapter Eight

Braun and Marie ate dinner in silence. Both people of few words, the growing intimacy they shared buoyed their closeness. The way Braun instinctively knew when Marie needed him to reach for her hand, the way he allowed her to freely speak her mind, to laugh, or cry when she needed spoke volumes to her. She didn't need constant mindless chatter between them to feel a deep connection to him. Braun's thoughts mirrored Marie's. He admired the way she was comfortable and confident in her own skin. Marie was exactly herself with him, she didn't play games and didn't expect him to, either. He abhorred pretense and found Marie to be refreshing and enlightened. In this moment they didn't need to discuss what was on their minds, it was obvious.

"Can we move my things in tonight?"

"Of course."

They spoke very little on the ride to the winery, but held hands the entire way. They were embarking on a new chapter of their lives and each one had their doubts. At the winery, Tilda watched in silence as Braun and Marie walked in. Just as Marie took the first step toward her room she spoke.

"Things have changed I see, Marie. Do you two need some supper then?"

"No, Tilda, we ate thank you. I'll be moving in with Braun, but I will make sure the Piano Technician's Association pays you my rent in full."

"Moving in together, this is news."

Braun and Marie did not respond and quickly took the stairs to Marie's room.

Tilda did not notice that Viktor had walked up behind her and when she turned around muttering to herself in Hungarian, she slammed into him.

"Move!" she shouted.

"Even you cannot stop fate Tilda. They are together for a reason. You should think about what you are doing now."

"What do you know, you coward. Is better that Illes family who think they are royalty own the letters and keep things secret. No, Budapest needs to know the truth."

"And you need the money, no? Don't think for one moment I am taken in by your false patriotism, you are a cunning old rat, but I know you. Budapest is not your first concern; we both know your black heart has no love in it for anyone, but yourself. I will do whatever I have to do to stop you and your secret thugs. Mark my words Tilda, I will."

Tilda spat in his face.

"Traitor!"

Braun and Marie packed what little possessions she had and started downstairs. When they reached the living room, she heard crying coming from one of the rooms off the garden.

"I have to check; it might be Viktor."

"I'm coming with you."

They stopped at Hans and Sarah's room. Hans was sobbing holding onto a picture of Sarah. Marie knocked gently.

"Hans, are you OK?"

"No, no I am not. She is gone, I know something bad will happen. I can't talk to you, I'm sorry." He tried to shut the door, but Braun's foot prevented him.

"Please, I cannot speak to you, she is in too much danger."

Marie and Braun walked into his room and shut the door. Braun put his hand on Han's shoulder.

"Tell us what's happening, we can help. Does it have anything to do with the letters? It's all right we know about them. You won't be in any trouble and maybe, we can find her."

"We have been in Hungary so long, my parents' faith in me is gone, no steady work, no friends to help. Miss Marie, the job you got me, it is all we have, and I am grateful. This opportunity came a few months ago, we thought it was a Godsend, the opportunity we'd been looking for. All we needed to do was keep it secret. We would help get letters, collect our pay, so much money enough to get us to America and buy a little farm. We would leave all the politics to them. But the secret meetings, the feeling I got from her new friend Agotha, I begged her, please don't go, nothing is worth losing you. I fear I've lost her already."

"Who is this Agotha?"

"They met in the library in the music listening room, another dancer. It seemed good for Sarah, but when I met her, I knew in my bones, she was Budapest slime, I knew it!"

"Where did Sarah go?"

"To a meeting. She didn't know where Agotha was taking her, but that car she drives will be easy to find. It's a wreck, smoke coming out the exhaust. I'm sure she took her to some run-down seedy street, there are a million in Budapest. How will we find her?"

"Did Sarah keep a diary, or a notepad? There could be a clue here. May we look?"

"Yes, yes of course, how stupid of me, I will look too."

The three of them scanned the large room and the bathroom examining anything that belonged to Sarah.

"Look!" Hans stood by the closet, holding one of Sarah's sweaters. In the pocket, he found a business card. It read, HHPS, Hungarian Historical Preservation Society, with an address scrawled on the back. It was not Sarah's handwriting, but it was a clue.

"Hans, let Marie and I handle this. You stay here in case Sarah returns. Here is my cell number, call if she comes back or if anyone contacts you with her whereabouts. Yes?"

"Yes, yes I'll do it. If you find her, you call me."

"Of course. We'll find her, I promise."

Braun and Marie left the winery in a hurry. Marie wondered if Braun knew something he wasn't sharing.

"Do you know where to go?"

"I have an idea. These people have been operating here for centuries. My family has kept an eye on them from a distance and they have done the same. It is why die Wächter was eventually formed. We needed to keep one step ahead of them at all times. The HHPS blame us and want nothing more than to see the old families of Budapest fall. In the beginning they were just a band of misfit scholars and musicians, harmless. But, over the years it has become a gang, a ruthless, violent gang. They care nothing about history anymore, it's just about money and perceived retribution against the wealthy families. It sickens me."

"But if it's dangerous, why are we going alone?"

"We are not alone. Trust me."

Braun pulled the car, head lights off, down a dark side street. When he cut the engine three other cars flashed their lights.

"Are those the members of die Wächter?"

"Yes. You should stay here; I do not know exactly what we are walking into."

"Right, nice try."

Marie followed Braun to the trunk of the car. He lifted the carpet and took out two handguns. He hesitated.

"Have you ever shot a gun before?"

"No, but that won't stop me from using it, I assure you."

Braun handed Marie the gun even though his insides were screaming at him not to.

"Promise you will stay near me, promise me, Marie."

"Yes, I promise."

The group assembled in a dark alleyway. They spoke in Hungarian, but Marie didn't protest. Braun and Marie stayed behind as the first and second groups started out. Braun kept pushing Marie behind him, always wanting his hand on her to know exactly where she was should he need to push her out of the way. It made Marie feel safe and annoyed at the same time.

Trust him, Marie.

Marie heard the command loud and clear and stopped walking causing Braun to stop as well and turn to her.

"What is it, what's wrong?" he whispered.

"Nothing, I'm sorry, let's keep on going."

Marie knew he had not heard it. Was it the piano, or was it Evangeline? She wasn't sure, but right now, she needed to stay near Braun, to stay sharp and to survive.

The house about two blocks up was mostly dark. A light could be seen in the back room and there were no cars out front. Marie noticed there was another structure behind the house. She couldn't make out if it was a shed or a doghouse. It was just too dark.

Braun stopped at the side of the house; the windows were covered with dark curtains so they could not see inside. The two groups arranged themselves to the left and right of the front door. The man in the lead held up his hand in a fist. Then slowly he raised one, two, three fingers. On the third finger ten men crashed through the front door and Marie could hear shouting and the pop of firearms. She held her breath.

A man shouted "Secure!" Marie and Braun went inside. Several men lay shot and bleeding on the ground, a woman is being handcuffed in the kitchen and two men with semi-automatic shot guns stood on the stairs.

"Did you find her?"

"No, she's not here."

Marie took Braun's hand and started to lead him out the side kitchen door.

"Hold up!" shouted one of the men. "We'll go with you."

The woman in the kitchen locked eyes with Marie and then dramatically tilted her head downward. Marie wasn't sure what it meant, but she felt sure she was trying to tell her something.

Outside, three men were in the small shed.

"There's no one here."

Marie scanned the earthen floor of the small shed, then something in the far-right corner caught her eye.

"Look!" She pointed to the corner. They aimed their flashlights on it and could see the dirt was sparce and what looked like the edge of a hatch door.

Quickly the men surrounded the space with light while two of then dug with their bare hands at the wood. Indeed, it was a hatch.

"Stand back," one of them whispered. Braun pulled Marie to the far-left corner and shielded her by placing his large body in front of her. "Don't move," he commanded.

The men ripped the door open and instantly shots rang out from below. Two men fired back and bravely descended the stairs. "Clear!" they shouted.

Braun and Marie carefully took the four steep steps to the earthen room below. Three men were dead on the ground and in the corner on a blood-soaked cot, lay Sarah.

The men shone their flashlights on her as Marie went to her side. She was gravely injured, but Marie could see she was alive, but just barely.

"I've got you; you are safe. Hold on Sarah, hold on, we will get you to a hospital."

Marie looked at Braun who was already on the phone giving directions to the ambulance. The men covered Sarah with blankets dropped down by those above and Marie held her hand for the four excruciatingly long minutes it took the ambulance to arrive.

Marie insisted they follow the ambulance and Braun agreed. A guard was posted at the entrance to the small hospital, at the entrance to the ICU ward and one at the door of Sarah's room. She was immediately taken to surgery.

"I should call Hans, but I am shaking."

"Let me."

Braun remained incredibly calm as he told Hans about Sarah. He offered to pick him up, but Hans had called his brother who was waiting with him at the winery. They would be there in ten minutes.

Braun and Marie waited in small waiting area off ICU. A kind nurse made them tea and the comfort of the warm cup in her hands and with Braun at her side, Marie began to breathe normally again. Hans arrived with his brother and Braun told him Sarah was in surgery and coaxed them to sit. Marie held his hand and promised they would help him and not leave them until Sarah was well.

It was four in the morning when the surgeon came into the small waiting room. He gently touched Marie's arm to wake her. Hans jumped up frantically talking gibberish. Marie took his arm and told the surgeon he was Sarah's husband.

"She is alive. We were able to repair the vocal cords, but the tissue was very damaged. Luckily, the knife went straight through and when they pulled it out, they did so at the same angle. Otherwise, she would have died instantly. She's lost a lot of blood and is very weak."

Hans fell into the chair, weeping. The surgeon put his hand on Han's shoulder and spoke.

"She made it through the surgery. She will live and, in a few days, we will know if the repair to her vocal cords will hold. Have hope young man. You can see her in the morning. For now, you should get some sleep. You two have a long road ahead. She will need you to be strong."

Marie, Braun, and Hans' brother Annish convinced Hans to go home. Annish agreed to stay with him, and Marie and Braun promised to check in on them in the morning.

"We need sleep, too." Braun took Marie's arm and led her to his car.

The morning light passed over their bed unseen and it wasn't until noon Braun stirred. He looked at Marie sleeping peacefully. He wanted her life to always be this way, peaceful, not dangerous, or violent. His love for her grew with each day they spent together, and he prayed he wouldn't end up in jail. Marie opened her eyes to see Braun staring at her.

"What is it? Did Hans call?"

"No, my love, relax."

"What's wrong then?"

"I have found you and for once I am afraid. I can't lose you, Meine Liebe."

To understand what is at stake, you must understand love. As much I despise Braun, he is one of us. He loves her, may God strike him dead if he does not keep her safe!

I loved our Therese Marie, and I loved my master. Beethoven and I feverishly composing as the rest of the world slept. Bittersweet years, his excruciating loneliness a constant companion which rose and set on him more often than the sun on the opera houses of Vienna. But I was there, always. The touch of his barrel like hands evoking music we both knew the likes of which had never been heard. He would laugh and pet me, his reliable tool and companion in a world that shunned him as the politics of favor rounded in and out like one of Strauss' flowery waltzes. Later, my helpless eyewitness account of his slow demise. When he died, I was left abandoned in a cottage and then taken to Liszt. Yes, I concede some say a maestro. Perhaps, but he paled in comparison to my master.

The great Van Beethoven would play me and what a workout it was! Such strong hands, such quick movement I thought sure I would come alive and dance in the room exultant. In his hands I was deft and luminous, bold, soft, and woeful, whatever he played I could respond. When he composed, I stayed in step with him never missing a note and when he struggled, I forced my voice to be as loud as possible so that he might feel the vibrations of my sound. I alone nurtured the master's passion so that he could finish his most famous works. Even when he became overwrought with grief and would pound his fists on my sides, I stayed firm in place, letting my body be his hair shirt, whatever he needed.

I understood his broken heart as a surgeon knows the winding course of invisible veins. Using the entirety of my body and soul, I recreated his emotions as he felt them sung by the notes he commanded. The music and I like faithful dogs giving unconditional love.

Our Therese Marie was a singular woman. Creative, bold, and talented. Did you not know this? Therese Marie played alongside him at my bench. They would play with the exuberance of children; she would create a melody and he would finish it. No other love ever existed like theirs, and it never will again.

This young Marie is his legacy, the chance to keep secret his one true love, the love he was able to keep to himself. A cruel secret for they could not have what every ordinary person is afforded. Love, marriage, and children. They could never marry, never live in the open. They were robbed of the simplest of human rights. Keeping the secret of their love meant no ridicule would befall them, no whispers in the street, no judgement by man, resigned God would do as he pleased; they were blessed only by the moon and the stars. His music, the only other passion of his heart, became the currency on which his place in this world was made. People expected the unconscionable of him. In their eyes, he was not fit to be loved because he could not be tamed. He always lived just outside of the realm of what people deemed excusable. Exposing his love for her would have left her destitute, made him an outcast, his music left to the whims of time. Like leaves in the wind, would his music scatter, decay, and be lost forever?

All he endured just to have love; it must not have been for naught; it cannot be so. I am desperate, Braun and Marie, they must prevail!

Chapter Nine

Marie's phone chirps breaking the hushed silence in Braun's house.

"It's Viktor, he says he needs to speak with us."

"I think we should meet him. I think Viktor knows something."

"I trust your instincts, Braun, let's meet him."

Mare and Braun arrive at the winery and meet Viktor in the courtyard just outside his room. His warm, firm embrace and easy manner with her and Braun, confirms for Marie, Viktor is a good man who knows something important.

"Thank you for coming, both of you. I have some information you need. I was waiting for the right moment, but now with poor Sarah in the hospital, I do not think I can wait any longer. I hope you will trust me. I assume you know the story of Zoltan Chernesvky?"

Braun nods his head yes and Marie notices the surprise in his face which he did not admit. *I must know him well*, she thought. The recognition in his face was barely perceptible unless you had studied every detail of his face, as she had.

"My great grandfather was a good friend of his. He came to our house many times. My father brought me into die Wächter at a young age which makes what I must tell you seem more dangerous. When I was young, I knew Tilda. She came from a dirt-poor family. We were poor too, but I am lucky. My family is loving, and kind and music was a constant light in our lives. Tilda's family were cruel people. Tilda and I, well, we did as young people do. We were not in love, but I cared for her, I wanted to help her. I was not successful in that endeavor. But what you need to know is this. I know her very well. She is deeply involved in the HHPS, and she arranged for you, my dear Marie, to come to Budapest."

Marie blushed with embarrassment.

"So, I wasn't really chosen for this job after all." Marie instantly regretted saying this out loud. She knew it was awkward for Braun, too.

"I believe you were, after all, they allowed your application to be approved. You are meant to be here in more ways than one, my dear."

Marie swallowed hard, now wasn't the time to be selfish. She could sort out what really happened with the appointment and her career later.

"Yes, I'm sorry, Viktor, please continue."

"Tilda is working to have the Illes family put in prison and to expose the letters. She knows Agotha and arranged the meeting where poor Sarah was almost killed. She's not here now of course, she knew I would not let her get away with it. She is in hiding somewhere."

"Thank you for being so frank with us, Viktor. Do you want us to find Tilda?"

"No, that coward will surface eventually. Right now, there is something more important we need to do. I'm glad you trust me because there is much more to know. We need to leave for Megyer as soon as you can."

"Megyer, there is nothing there."

"I'm glad you think so. We hope the HHPS thinks so, too."

"Megyer is a tiny remote village west of Budapest, Meine Liebe. As far as I know, there is no connection to Beethoven, but I can see our friend Viktor knows otherwise. We drove here in my sports car; we will return with my SUV and leave in about an hour."

"Don't delay, I'll be waiting."

The drive to Megyer was slow due to unmaintained country roads. Viktor said very little about why they were headed to one of the most remote villages outside Budapest. Marie googled the town and was surprised to learn it has a population of only about two hundred people. She trusted Viktor, but still, the idea of she and Braun being so far outside the city in a remote area still seemed liked a risky thing to do. She glanced down at Braun's phone which was on silent and noticed he had been in touch with his fellow die Wächter members. They would not be alone. Marie took a deep breath and squeezed Braun's hand.

"Take this next turn off, here on the right."

Braun did as Viktor instructed. They were now on a dirt road, rolling hills and meadows as far as the eye could see. A few miles later, Marie noticed wood fences lining the road on either side, an indication the property was owned and maintained. She fidgeted in her seat, anxious for what came next. Braun took her hand to calm her.

"We are almost there, don't worry, everything is going to be all right."

Marie was grateful to Viktor, there was something about him; she instinctively felt safe with him. She hoped her instincts were right.

The dirt road finally ended at a pretty farmhouse with potted flowers out front, chickens running here and there, and Marie noticed the yellow front door. So bright and happy, it seemed out of place considering what they were all involved in. There was something else, Marie was sure she'd seen this farmhouse, and the yellow door before. But how could she? She put the thought away for now anxious to find out why they were here.

As they got out of Braun's SUV, a man came walking slowly from the backyard of the cottage.

"Ah, Ivan, you are still alive I see."

Marie noticed a certain coldness pass between the two men, but said nothing. She wondered what had transpired between them.

"You will mourn my death then Viktor? These must be the friends you told me about."

Marie stuck out her hand first.

"Hello, I'm Marie and this is Braun."

"Marie, my dear you look just like her."

Ivan embraced Marie tightly and held her for longer than she expected. Marie waited, knowing he should be the one to pull away first.

"Braun Illes, I am pleased to meet you. I know your family well."

Braun remained silent, but Marie was not surprised. Braun was an observer first; he never jumped in to fill in the pauses in conversation and he was a skeptic. Marie understood why given all that his family had been through. She let the silence fall between them and did not interject.

"I'm sure you have questions, and you want to get to the reason my friend brought you here. Follow me."

Ivan led them behind the house and stopped at an old garden shed. He picked up a shovel from inside and resumed walking into the bramble of trees and bushes. Beyond the thicket of trees, they emerged into a small clearing. Ivan walked a few paces ahead and stopped.

"I think you should do the honors, Miss Marie."

Before Braun could protest, Marie took the shovel.

"Right about here, please." Ivan motioned for her to dig.

Marie could see Braun was not happy about this situation, but she flashed him a smile and wink and he seemed to settle, at least for the moment.

Marie dug for only a few minutes when she heard the distinct thud of the shovel hitting wood. She looked at Braun.

"It's all right, Miss Marie, just once more, lightly and you will have found the box."

Marie did as she was instructed. She was so curious and excited, before she realized it, she was on her knees using her hands to brush dirt away from the box.

When the box was visible to all, she stopped.

Ivan motioned for her to open it. Marie traced the outline of the box with her hand and found the hinge, a

103

little further around she found the front and gingerly opened the box. Letters, just like the ones the man in the library gave her and the ones Braun had. She sat back in the grass and removed them from the box and pressed them to her chest.

The group was silent. Marie put the letters back in the box.

"I'd like to read them later, if that's OK."

"Now might be a good time for tea, yes?"

As they made their way back to the house, Marie slid her hand around Braun's waist. She needed to be near him, to feel protected. He instinctively held her close to his side and they rounded the trail back to the cottage.

Ivan led them inside. It is a comfortable, sunny place and he told them to sit at the wood table in the kitchen while he put the kettle on to boil.

Marie asked if she could use the bathroom to wash her hands and Ivan led her down the short hallway. The small window in the bathroom let in a stream of light and the faded handmade curtains rustled in the breeze. Marie touched the curtains and felt a strange sensation in her chest. Overcome with emotion, she wiped tears away from her eyes.

When she returned tea had been poured, biscuits were laid out on an old china plate and the room felt serene as if they were old friends making a Sunday visit.

"I'm very glad you are here today Marie and Braun. Viktor has told me of what is occurring and about that poor young girl in the hospital. I pray for her recovery. I have a little story to tell, and I think it may help clear some things up for you, my dear."

Marie laid her hand on Braun's, ready to hear whatever Ivan had to share.

"It was so long ago; I was much younger, and I think more handsome then." He said with an easy laugh.

Viktor made a rude coughing sound and got up from his seat.

"Evangeline was the love of my life, dear Marie. I know you did not know this, but it's important you do now. She and I weathered many hard times including her brief affair with her cousin. But, we prevailed, our love prevailed and when she learned she was carrying you, I knew I would have to decide. Do I love her enough to live without her most of the time? I knew she would stay in America until you were out of college. She and I would have scant moments together for most of our lives. I could have abandoned her and went on with my life. But, I could not abandon her; she was my one true love. We saw each other whenever she could visit, she brought me pictures of you as you grew. I knew you were the other love of her life. When I learned she was close to death, I made plans to travel to America to see her for the last time. She died before I left. But on her last visit here, she made me promise to look out for you and to make sure you never fell prey to the HHPS. She knew you would find your way to Hungary, and I knew I would find a way to help you when it mattered most. Today is that day."

Marie is sobbing, Braun pulls her chair very close to him and puts his arm around her. She doesn't care if these three men see her weep, she had good reason to cry. She loved her aunt, her mother, and mourned the fact she never got to share in this part of her life. Her emotions were coming to the surface, but for once, she let it be. She let herself feel and she knew Braun would be there for her.

"When I learned the letters had been given to the consulate by the vile HHPS, I needed no prodding to take action. At one time, I held a high position in the government. I knew where the most secret and precious documents were stored. I started working long hours so the others saw it as routine for me. I'm a patient man, after five months, no one commented about it anymore, my new hours just folded into the daily habit of our work. I stole the letters from the lock up room and buried them. They have been hidden here for over two years. The only other person who knows this, is my friend Viktor, a fellow patriot."

Braun asked the obvious question, "But how did you get away with it, they must have questioned everyone? They knew you had access, correct?"

"I did not have access as you say, but I had knowledge of where they were kept, and I knew where the keys were stowed. The person in charge of the sealed room was a drunk, we all knew it. I knew he left at precisely four in the afternoon every day to meet his friends at the pub one town over. Sometimes, he would be in such a hurry, he left the keys in the desk. I made a copy with some wax. A few nights later I used my copy to retrieve the letters, letters which were never their property to have."

"You were always the brave one, Ivan."

Viktor was looking out the kitchen door as he spoke. He seemed disconnected to the rest of the group.

"They suspected many people, but in truth, they never suspected me. They asked me to help with the interrogation of those they did have cause to suspect. Of course, I was happy to help and did my job well."

Braun had to chuckle a bit at this. As with many things in government, time manages to sweep away the conflict and life goes on. Braun wished with everything in his soul the government would forget about the letters and the HHPS but, that was far too much to ask for.

"These letters belong to you, Marie. You can take them, or we can bury them again, leave them here until you feel it is safe to have them. I am your loyal servant, just as I was to Evangeline."

"Thank you, Ivan, and Viktor, I am overwhelmed right now, but I am eternally grateful for your friendship and someday Ivan, I would like to know more about you and Evangeline. It's a part of her life I know nothing about, but I would like to, if you are willing."

"Of course, Marie, it would be my pleasure. You and Braun, are welcome here, any time."

"I have to ask, Ivan, was it you who gave me two letters in the library?"

"Ah, yes it was. Forgive me for being so secretive, but I avoid being seen in public in Budapest. I worked in the government for over forty years, too many people would recognize me there."

"I understand."

Marie stared at the letters, quietly lost in her own thoughts. The men talked but she did not hear a word. She felt sure she knew something about Ivan from Evangeline, but could not pinpoint it. A nagging feeling told her Evangeline had given her clues, clues she missed because she was too absorbed in her own life and her career. She glanced at the peeling yellow paint on the front door which was left open. Bees buzzed at the flowers and the birds softly trilled. Then, it hit her. Memories flooded her mind. She pushed her chair back with her legs at stood up.

"A picture. She carried a picture of the two of you in her wallet her whole life. I must have looked at it a hundred times. The yellow door, I remember it. You two standing in front of it, your arm around her, she looked so happy. She told me you were her twin, the mirror of herself. It makes sense now, she couldn't tell me she loved you, she would have had to tell me the entire story."

"Meine Liebe, I'm glad you remembered."

"You are right, Marie. Evangeline and I spent many happy days here in my house. She loved being here away from the city, away from the prying eyes of people in both our lives. This place was our sanctuary, our hideaway. She came as often as she was able."

Viktor abruptly grabbed his hat and jingled the car keys in his pocket. Braun, feeling the air of tension, decided it was a good time to leave.

"It's getting late, we should get back to Budapest."

Marie picked up his cue.

"Yes, Braun is right. Ivan, I'd like you to keep them buried, here, for now, if you don't mind. I don't think they will be safe with Braun or me, the HHPS have eyes on us all the time. I will be in touch with you when it is safe to retrieve them. I can't thank you enough Ivan."

"Of course, Marie, whatever you wish. We are here for you, old Viktor, and I, we are at your disposal."

Marie chooses to sit in the backseat alone on the ride back to Budapest. She can't help, but think of Evangeline. Were there more clues to her life away from Boston she missed? Marie remembered while she was in grad school, Evangeline spent more and more time in Hungary. Was this when she met Braun's father? Marie would house sit and care for the current bevy of stray cats her aunt took in and she would keep the house plants alive. Marie did not realize Evangeline was ill until very late in her treatment. It was when she returned home from one of her last trips to Hungary Marie noticed something was very wrong. At the airport, Marie was shocked to see one of the airline hosts pushing her in a wheelchair. Evangeline was pale and thin; she was too weak to speak. Marie held back her tears as she drove back to their house, Evangeline asleep in the backseat.

"Here aunt, drink this tea, and I will bring you some soup."

"Meine Liebe, we should talk."

"But you should rest now, we can talk later.

"I will rest later, but please sit with me. I need to talk to you."

Marie pulled the rocking chair close to Evangeline's bed. She took her frail hand as tears escaped her eyes.

"Oh, Aunt, I'm not ready to let you go."

"I'm not ready to go my love, but the Gods have other plans. You must listen to me now. Your life will be beautiful and filled with love Meine Liebe, but only if you learn to trust someone, let someone close to you. Go to Hungary, promise me you will go."

"But why should I go there?"

"Ah, I don't have the strength right now to tell you everything, but I know your destiny is there. Please, trust me, say you do, promise."

"Of course, I trust you, don't worry, I promise, I will go. Now please, get some rest, we'll talk more later."

Marie left her aunt to sleep and wept leaning on the kitchen counter. She had one more semester at Berklee before she published her PhD., the last thing on her mind right now. Just as her life was about to begin, she would lose the one person in the world who really knew her and loved her. How would she go on?

In the soft hours of dusk, Marie carefully climbed the stairs with a bowl of soup for her aunt. She found her unresponsive in bed and called an ambulance. As she waited, Marie knelt by Evangeline's side and held her hand. Just before the EMT's banged on the front door, Evangeline opened her eyes.

"Marie, forgive me…"

The EMT's rushed to her, but Evangeline was pronounced dead within a few minutes. Marie's heart broke into a thousand pieces. She had called her mother and father the day before to let them know Evangeline was dying, but there was no return phone call. After the EMT's and the coroner left the house, Marie called them again and this time, when she left a message, she did not hold back.

"Evangeline is dead, not that you care. I now know if it was me who died, you would not have come to see me either. I want you both to know how disappointed I am in you, that you failed miserably as parents and family for me and her. You should be ashamed of yourselves. I'm planning her send-off per her wishes. If you call back, I might let know what they are."

Marie hung up and in that very moment, she cut the cord that tethered her to parents she hardly knew, people she did not love anymore. Evangeline's attorney came to visit Marie about a week later with her aunt's will. Marie had no idea what was in it. Having never heard back from her parents except for a sympathy card in mail, signed with their names, but no message, Marie met with the attorney by herself. Evangeline had some money and of course, she left it all to Marie, the townhouse they lived in, her beloved yellow Karmann Ghia, and a letter which Marie put away to read another day.

The house was lonely without Evangeline. Marie finished her PhD, acting on autopilot, she wondered how she ever got through it. She kept the townhouse and loved living in it. She landed a decent job working for a branch of the International Association of Piano Builders and Technicians, her work was satisfying, but she was getting restless. Boston was home, but she'd grown tired of the city, and she never found a partner, she never came close to experiencing mad, passionate love. Since Evangeline died there was a gap in her life that seem to widen with each passing year.

Marie was ready for a change and began looking for the next step in her career. That's when the request from the Hungarian National Museum arrived. It felt like Evangeline had made it so. Marie applied for the job right away. When she got the call from the museum curator, she did not hesitate to accept. *Thanks, Aunt, I know you want me to go and so I am.* Marie hired a house sitter and made plans to leave Boston within the month. She brought the unopened letter from her aunt's will with her. Maybe, she would have the guts to read it, or maybe, she would wait.

Chapter Ten

Marie's phone rings jolting her out of her memories. It's Hans; she puts him on speaker.

"Hans, is there any news?"

"Yes, Sarah is awake, thank God. She cannot speak yet; the doctors aren't saying much about her chances, but they say to keep hope. Oh, Miss Marie, I am so grateful to you and Braun, she is alive, my Sarah is alive."

Hans is weeping again so Marie winds up the call and lets him know they will visit when they get back to Budapest. The long drive back is difficult. The traffic around the city is crazy, tourist season in Hungary. Marie and Braun drop Viktor off at the winery and decide to call it a night and visit Sarah in the morning.

Thanks to Braun's butler, dinner is waiting for them at his house, the fireplaces are lit, and both Braun and Marie are glad to be home. Marie yawns as she eats, the drive, the emotions of the day weighed on her.

"Why don't you take a bath, come to bed when you are done. My house is your home now. You should feel free to take time for yourself, to relax and enjoy the comforts we have."

"Have I mentioned how lucky I am? I would love a long soak. Braun, thank you."

Braun is confident enough in himself to give Marie the space she needs, she feels more certain everyday she has found her soul mate. The warm water in the large marble tub is heavenly; scented with lavender oil and bergamot, like being at a spa. Braun certainly knows how to treat a woman. The room is lit with candles, and it is quiet, so blissfully quiet Marie can think. Her mind replays the events of the day. Digging up the letters felt like therapy. Digging, an apt metaphor for her time here, digging at her past, digging at her soul to allow Braun to love her, and digging into the history of the Broadwood, the piano who will not be silenced. Ever since she arrived in Hungary, she's had to pull away the surface layers of so much. Secrets, hidden love, and Braun. In just two short months her life has spun off its axis and the ride has been dizzying. She closes her eyes and breathes deeply, relaxing for the first time in a long time.

Marie dresses in comfortable clothes and pulls her hair into a loose bun. She meets Braun in the drawing room where he is talking to the butler.

"I thought maybe, you crawled into bed by now."

"I am tired, but I am so curious. Part of me wishes I took the letters, but I meant what I said. It would only put both of us in more danger. I feel safe here with you, I don't want anything to spoil that."

"Keeping you safe is all I care about. Are you coming up?"

"In a minute, I'd like to sit by the fire for a little while."

Marie hoped Braun would sense she needed to be alone with her thoughts.

"Of course, goodnight, my love."

That man has a knack with women, Marie thought. *Hard to believe he's never been in. love before.* Marie settles in by the fire and soon, the warm fire, the smooth whiskey makes her sleepy.

Marie hears Braun's footsteps coming fast down the stairs.

"Miene Liebe, I am sorry, I need to tell you something."

"What is it, what's wrong."

"It's Tilda, she tried to kill Sarah at the hospital."

"What?"

"Apparently, she was able to bribe the police guards and managed to get into Sarah's room. She was going to inject her with a street version of epinephrine to stop her heart. Luckily, one of the nurses saw her and yelled for help. She and three other nurses were able to stop her. Tilda was arrested and taken to jail."

"Sarah, is she OK?"

"Yes, she is fine. Tilda was not successful."

"I want to be there when they question her."

"So do I but, Braun, I highly doubt that's possible."

"You may be right, but I'm going to try."

***

The next morning, the police station is bustling with pickpockets and Americans who refused to obey traffic laws arguing over fines. Braun finds his friend, a Chief Master Sargent who is not assigned to Tilda's case, but has pull within ranks of the Rendőrsége (The Hungarián National Polcié) and Interpol.

Braun's friend Lajos leads him to a small interrogation room.

"Wait here. When they bring her in for questioning, you can see and hear everything from here, but you cannot speak to her. I'm sorry Braun, they have this case under tight security, I have no pull. But at least you will know what she says."

"Thank you, Lajos, you are a true friend and patriot."

Tilda is brought in and shoved into a straight-backed metal chair. Two police guards sit opposite her, another stands at attention in the corner near the door.

"Let me out of here you slime. I've done nothing wrong, but try to save our history."

The police guard snaps on the recorder as he speaks.

"Mrs. Tilda Uzcheck, is that your name, for the record."

"You know my name, traitors!"

"Ms. Uzcheck, if you refuse to cooperate, you will rot in a jail cell until you do. The Hungarian prison has many beds, you are welcome to one for as long as *we* like, understand?"

"What do want to know that you don't already know, idiot."

"Why did you try to kill Sarah Kovacks in the Budapest General Hospital yesterday?"

Tilda does not speak right away. She scans the room, looks at the two-way window, gets out of her chair and stands in front of it, her nose at the glass. She spits on it.

"I know you are listening Braun Illes, scum of Budapest royalty. Keep listening and one day you too, will die."

"Sit down!"

The police guard at the door grabs Tilda under her arm so hard she squeals. He easily lifts her off the floor as he walks. He puts her in back in her chair and handcuffs her hands behind her back.

"Thank you, David. You will sit here, like that, until you tell us what we want to know. You have no advantages here Ms. Uzcheck."

"You want to know where the last letter is mighty Braun Illes? Ha! You think everyone at your museum is under your control. We know the truth because we have it firsthand from someone right under your nose. Ask her, ask your old lover."

Tilda spews a long, crazy laugh. Braun has heard enough. He leaves the interrogation room and walks out of the station. Outside, he leans on the building, catching his breath. Tilda just implicated someone on his staff, someone close. He knows who she is talking about, it can only be Hanna.

Braun needs to talk to Hanna and quickly. But he knows he must handle this delicately and he can't tell Marie, at least not yet. His stomach turns at the thought. Marie does not know about Hanna and telling her now would feel like betrayal no matter how hard he tried to explain. There can be no other choice. He must talk to Hanna; he must find out what she has done.

Chapter Eleven

Ah, Hanna, I knew he would have to confront his past sooner or later. She is like a spool of thread, tied to him, tied to me; long, tangled threads of regret. Her heart beats only for that fool but she holds the key, the last letter. I have watched her weep for him and heard the pounding of the blood in her veins whenever he draws near. If she betrays him, she betrays us all. Hear me Hanna, you must obey!

Braun's phone chirps with a text from Marie. He stares at her name. How can he lie to her? He loves her with all his heart and soul, a first for him. For now, he must contain his emotions. There will be time later to explain why he did not tell her about his connection to Hanna. He texts back a reply, a lie saying he needed to meet with the museum board giving him ample time to talk to Hanna.

Braun takes the long way back to the museum. He thinks about Hanna and his youth. Hanna Toth, curator of antiquities at the Hungarian National Museum is as close as a family member could be to the Illes family except that she is not in fact, family. Her family descended from Hungarian royalty, and they have been very close with the Illes family since the seventeenth century. She and Braun shared a friendship more akin to cousins; they grew up together. He trusted her and she trusted him.

Braun never felt for Hanna the way he feels for Marie. But he and Hanna were close, and she was beautiful then. Braun was attracted to her, and he felt safe with her; they grew up together. Braun and Hanna had a brief but intense affair. He left her to study in Vienna and he never wrote to her except when he wrote to his family and sent "his regards" her way. Braun suspected Hanna felt more for him than he could return. A constant undercurrent, it was always there, each ignored it in their own way, but sometimes, Braun sensed Hanna wanted to change it, she wanted to be with him.

Hanna's private rooms on the top floor of the museum have been her home for over ten years. It is also the floor where the Broadwood is temporarily housed in a temperature controlled, vault-like room. She sits in her favorite chair by the fireplace, a glass of wine nearby. She pulls a wool blanket over her knees and settles herself. After a few sips of wine, she opens the small drawer in the side table. Carefully, she reaches in and takes out the letter. She holds it gingerly like a fragile glass flower. Slowly, gently, she unfolds it to read the words she's read a thousand times before. The letter is hers, it is her talisman of sorts, a bittersweet reminder of the fragility of love. The last letter, letter number eighteen in the lost letters to the Immortal Beloved.

January 1827

I cannot bear the thought of what is coming, my love. I long for you and yet I cannot bear to see you or touch your sad, beautiful face. You will be gone from me soon, and I will have to say my last goodbye. How can you leave this earth? How can such a force be silenced?

The child inside me stirs as I write. I will be lost until we are together again. I will raise our child to know his father loved him, and he will make you very proud.

But the music in my heart will stop. Blood will run in my veins, but I will not feel love again. How I wish I could go with you!

I am broken, I am betrayed. Gods be damned.

My love for you knows no earthly boundaries

Yours

Beethoven died two months after the last letter was written. The Immortal beloved would receive no reply and every time Hanna reads it, she weeps. Forbidden love. Something she knew a lot about. Hanna feels a deep kinship with the Immortal Beloved and Beethoven. She talks to the Broadwood late at night when she cannot sleep. She plays it, knowing it is against the rules, she makes sure to turn off the security cameras. The piano speaks to her. She feels his loneliness like a hollow echo, a call in the vast forest which goes unanswered.

Hanna folds the letter and places it back in the drawer. She lets out a long sigh and closes her eyes. Braun, so much he does not know. Hanna couldn't help herself. With her access to the security cameras, she watched Marie and

Braun together when they talk in the office. She also watched footage of the night they made love in the antique instrument room. Braun turned one of the cameras to the wall, but he did not know about the new camera she installed under the desk. In the early years when Braun took over management of the museum, he was gone most of the time. Hanna had to make some decisions without him and investing in security was important. She wasn't sorry.

She remembered his touch and the way he made love, a slow burn that turned into a wildfire. She was upset at first, but then why should she be? It was so long ago and even though they were not lovers, they were friends and he always treated her with respect and kindness. Still, she couldn't help, but be jealous of Marie, her talent, her beauty, and the fact that she was the only woman in the world that Braun wanted to marry. She knew in her heart Braun would marry Marie; it was just a matter of time. She wondered if she still had time to turn his head. *Nagy*, she laughed out loud to herself, the Hungarian word for lust. Braun used to tell her he could sum up their relationship in one word, *Nagy*. Perhaps, some of that still lingered.

Braun takes the elevator to the top floor, adjusts his sport coat, and takes a deep breath. He must play this cool. He cannot ambush Hanna; he must wind his way slowly to the question of the last letter. Like a crab on the shore, he must skirt around the main reason he is here, make her feel comfortable and then bring up the letters. Braun was nervous, ever since Marie was hired, he and Hanna seemed to be at odds over everything.

Reluctantly, he rings the bell at her door.

"Braun, this is a surprise. Are you firing me, or closing the museum?"

"Neither Hanna, can't an old friend visit another old friend?"

"Indeed, he can. He just never does, come in."

"Brandy, whiskey, what can I get you?"

"Whiskey, neat, please."

Drinks in hand, they settle in chairs opposite one another by the fire.

"So, why are you here, old friend?"

"You know you are my best friend Hanna, since we were three years old. You are important to me. I thought I was important to you, too. But lately, you don't even offer me the courtesy of an acquaintances in the street. You do not say good morning or goodbye, you don't visit me in the office. I wonder what has changed."

Hanna stares at the fire and doesn't speak right away. She is fighting with herself; should she run to him and beg him to make love to her, or should she play along with this cat and mouse game. She knows the reason he is here; he wants to tell her about Marie. She shifts in her chair as her thoughts shift as well. They have no relationship she reminds herself, they haven't for over thirty years. But he is her best friend, he is kind to her, she shouldn't fault him for finding love. They are also patriots caught in a dangerous fight to save the legacy of Beethoven for Budapest. Still, she deserves some leeway to taunt him, after all, she cannot change what was.

"Braun, I am woman, you remember that I assume?"

"Of course."

"Well, as a woman, it is my right to be jealous. There, I said it out loud. You have been mine all these years in a certain sense, you and I share a closeness. Since Marie came, I do not see you, you do not have a drink with me or dinner. I don't get to flirt with you and dream when I close my eyes about the old days, anymore. It's clear she has stolen your heart. What do you expect of this woman, of me, now?"

"Hanna, you will always be special to me, you know that. We have shared our whole lives. We had our time, no?"

"Ha, no we did not, not really, Braun. I'm sorry, but you asked."

Silence fell between them, but it was not uncommon for them to sit in silence together, the companionable silence of old friends. Hanna was right, they had shared their whole lives together, they were bonded. And it's true, Braun let her flirt with him sometimes coming very close to sleeping together, he is only human after all. But when he met Marie, it changed in an instant. He understood why she felt left out, he was guilty of disappearing from her life.

"Hanna, I am sorry. I am guilty of what you say. I do love Marie; I cannot lie to you. But it does not mean I don't care for you, and I always will. You know me, you know I am deeply in love, or I would not be with her. Old friend, you know me, I couldn't bear it if you never forgave me for being who I am."

"Ah Braun, I know, I knew before you walked in my door this is what you wanted to tell me. I hear you; I accept it. But don't shut me out, you enrage me when you do that."

"I won't, Hanna. Thank you, my sweet friend. But, there is something else."

Braun could see Hanna was surprised. He had to be careful.

"Something else? Like what?"

"Tilda Uzheck was arrested yesterday for trying to kill Sarah Kovacks."

"Is she OK?"

"Yes, Tilda was stopped in time. Sarah was unharmed."

Silence. Hanna knew what would come next. Her skin was crawling, she knew better than to lie to Braun, especially now after they had been so truthful with each other. Truthful to a point, Hanna still had secrets she wanted to keep from Braun.

Hanna had been kept up to date on the actions of the HHPS by a colleague in parliament. She knew they were active again, that Sarah was almost killed, and she also knew about Viktor and Ivan. She knew Marie now possessed all the letters kept hidden by die Wächter except for the last one, the one she had.

As was the case so often in her life, there were two sides to this situation at war in her heart. One, the letter itself, the letter she felt a deep kinship with. Forbidden love and a secret child. It's all she had, and it mirrored her own life. Especially, now she was sure Braun would marry

Marie and she would never be with him, she wanted to hold onto the letter. She felt sure it was meant for her alone to keep, to take to her grave, a shared legacy. But she is Hungarian and was taught to put the needs of the self behind doing what is right for your country.

Hanna was twenty-three when she realized she was pregnant with Braun's child. The result of a brief liaison when he came home for two months after his father died, his senior year of university. She made an excuse to visit Paris and an old friend for a couple months in the spring of 1994 and had an abortion. She never told Braun about the child. Unlike the Immortal Beloved, Hanna had choices. Braun's feelings would never match hers and when she thought about what their future together would look like under those circumstances, she could not allow it. Neither one of them would be happy, and she would be stripped of her independence, something she would not give up.

Second, there is the HHPS. She agreed to see them, to hear them out knowing it was a deep betrayal of her family, of Braun, and her country which she dearly loved. The HHPS offered her wealth beyond her wildest dreams, and the promise she would be the one to tell the story to the newspapers and the media. They would see to it she took over management of the museum, she would have the love of her people for giving them the chance to know Beethoven through his letters. She could tell the story of the Immortal Beloved in her own way, exhibit the letters in the museum. She would be the hero of her age in Budapest.

"You are very quiet Hanna, talk to me."

"I don't know what to say. What do you want?"

Braun put his glass down and went to Hanna. He knelt at her side, his hand on her knee. A bold move, but it is something he had done so many times before. He hoped the familiarity of the gesture would touch her heart, make her relent, and give the letter to him.

"You know we are the keepers, die Wächter; we cannot allow the HHPS to prevail. Hanna, you have always been my partner in this. You must give Marie the last letter."

Hanna wanted to rage at Braun, but looking into his eyes, those clear sky-blue eyes that know her so well, she melted. Sobbing, she spoke.

"I have nothing else now. The letter is mine, it's mine because it's my story, a story no one knows. The Immortal Beloved, I think she knows, we share the curse of forbidden love and a secret child. If I give them to Marie, she will have everything, she will have you and my letter. You are asking me to rip out my heart."

"A secret child?"

"Yes, my dear Braun. A long time ago when you were at university, you came home when your father died, we made love in these rooms, precious few times, but still, nights I cherished. I became pregnant, but I knew you didn't love me; you were not desperately in love with me, and time would not change it. And truthfully, I never wanted to be a mother, I certainly was not prepared to raise a child alone or with a man who did not love me. I had an abortion in Paris, I'm sorry. I should have told you, but what good would it have done?"

Braun stared into Hanna's eyes. She was important to him; she had a piece of his heart, and she was right about everything. He is a grown man now, he could not deny a child would have altered the course of their lives, and he did not love her, not like he loves Marie. He no longer possessed the bravado of a young man, he knew better. He took Hanna in his arms and let her cry. She needed him and he wanted to help her.

Standing by the elevator, Braun thanked Hanna for giving him the letter. They held hands and stood in silence for a moment. As Hanna pulled Braun to her, her lips locking on his, the elevator's soft chime sounded. The door opened and Marie watched as Braun and Hanna shared their last kiss.

Chapter Twelve

Marie pressed the button to close the elevator door just as Braun reached for her. She held her sides and winced. She felt like throwing up. The elevator seemed to be taking a thousand years to reach the first floor of the museum so she could make her exit. She would take a taxi to Braun's throw her things in a suitcase and head to the airport. She did not need to be involved in this crazy situation, and she certainly did not need to be in love with a man who could not be trusted. Her heart was shattering like glass as she clutched her sides. Finally, the elevator door opened, and Marie took off like a shot to the revolving doors at the front of the museum.

She ran into the street waving her arm like a crazy person. Finally, a taxi stopped. Marie got into it and rattled off Braun's address as the driver sped away. Lost in her thoughts wiping away tears that would not stop, and trying to breathe so she wouldn't throw up in the taxi, she was not paying attention to the driver who was talking to her. When she finally looked up, she recognized the man driving the car. It was Viktor.

"Viktor? Why are you here?"

"My dear, don't be alarmed and please do not be angry. I only want to help. Let me take you for a drink, yes?"

"Viktor, I appreciate it but, I have to leave here. I don't want to spend another moment in Budapest."

"I have felt the same way many times. But you need a friend, I am your friend Marie, you have more people here who care about you than you know. One drink and if you still want to leave, I will drive you to the airport myself."

Marie felt trapped, but she was devastated, and Viktor was so kind. She did need a friend and a drink.

"OK, one drink."

The restaurant was quiet and warm, and they seemed to know Viktor. Marie wasn't surprised, it seemed everyone was connected here, another reason to detest Budapest. Viktor led her to a secluded booth and as they settled in, he took her hand.

"What happened to make you so sad, you can tell me."

"Really, it doesn't matter. But what does matter is I don't want to be involved in this any longer. I want to go home."

"Some would say you are home, why do you want to leave?"

"I let myself become too attached to Budapest, to Beethoven's legacy, to the letters, to… Braun. It was a big mistake and now, I want to leave and never come back."

"Ah, Braun, Marie, will you permit me to tell you something?"

"OK."

"Braun is a good man. I know, I know you are hurt. But I can guess it has to do with Hanna, yes?"

"How did you know?"

"Theirs is an old story, and a dead one, that is the truth. They grew up together, their families linked by blood, duty, and fate. They were close once when they were young. She loved him, yes, but he did not love her, not in that way. He cares for her now like a sister. He loves you more than the air he breaths, this I know."

"Well, in America, we don't French kiss our sisters and brothers, maybe, it's different here, it wouldn't surprise me."

"You are hurt, I know. Maybe, what you saw was not as it appeared. Maybe, it was goodbye."

"Convenient theory. They can kiss hello and goodbye all they want. I'm out of the picture starting now. Viktor, you have been nothing, but kind to me, but this is all too much for me to handle. I feel so alone, I have nowhere to go here. I moved in with Braun, and I cannot be there with him now. I am a stranger in a strange land."

"And you need somewhere to hide for a while, yes?"

"Exactly."

"I have the place. Go to Megyer, Ivan will have no problem letting you stay as long as you like. You know you will be safe there. I will not tell Braun, although at some point, he will figure it out."

Marie was completely overwhelmed, her head pounded, her heart ached, and she desperately wanted to be alone. She could try to find a hotel, but most likely only the outrageously expensive ones were still available this time of year. She was running out of money and once the Piano

Technicians of America found out she wasn't working, she'd be cut off immediately. Reluctantly, she agreed.

"OK, maybe, just for a few days so I can think."

Marie excused herself to go the ladies' room while Viktor ordered some food. The Ladies room was empty, and Marie was grateful. She washed her face and hands and sat in an overstuffed chair near the door and let herself relax. She had to pull herself together and think, she needed to understand what was happening. In truth, she did not want to let the letters go, she cared about what happened to them, to Beethoven's legacy and of course, to Braun. She allowed herself a moment of pity, but decided there was so much more at stake for her here, she knew this chapter of her life was not over, and she accepted it. She knew she possessed the strength to handle this if she could let her ego go, something she had started to do the moment she let Braun love her.

Marie took one last look in the mirror, and as she reached for the handle of the door, it swung open and knocked her on the floor. A man pulled her up and shoved a rag laced with ether to her nose. She passed out within seconds.

Viktor sat patiently at the table as the waiter brought the food he ordered and two more drinks. He picked at the food, drank some of his wine when a sudden fear rose in his stomach. Marie! He ran to the ladies' room and found Marie's phone on the floor and her plaid wool scarf. She was gone, they had taken her.

Viktor called Braun immediately and his comrades in the die Wächter. They would meet at Braun's house and hatch a plan. There was no mistake, Marie was taken by the HHPS, and her life is in danger.

Chapter Thirteen

Braun is frantic, his usual composure dissolving into panic and rage. He is pacing in front of the fireplace when Viktor arrives.

"What happened, tell me everything, now."

"Of course, but you need to calm down, we have to keep our heads…"

"Tell me!"

"She left your house for the museum. Your butler called me as you instructed, and I found her in the street waving frantically for a taxi. She was so upset, crying, and choking in the back seat. I convinced her to let me take her for a drink. She said she wanted to leave Budapest and you, behind forever. I don't know why exactly, but I'm guessing you do."

"This is all my fault, damn it!"

"Now, you tell me, what happened at the museum, was Hanna, no?"

"I went to see Hanna, yes, to ask her for the last letter to give to Marie. I felt sorry for her. When I was leaving, Hanna kissed me. Marie was coming out of the elevator and saw us. It meant nothing, Viktor, you know I am telling the truth."

"Yes, I know, but Marie does not and now they have her. We have to act fast."

The other members of the die Wächter arrived and assembled in Braun's drawing room. Two women moved the coffee table and unzipped computer bags containing computers, two large monitors, a myriad of cords, and headphones.

"I have surveillance on Igor's car and Andras car as well, the two leaders of the HHPS. If they kidnapped Marie, these two are involved. The others gathered around the two women at the computer screens. A GPS tracking map appeared on the two screens.

One of the women pointed to the screen on the left.

"Here there they are. Since they are moving together, they must be on their way to rendezvous with the slime that have Marie. The western edge of the river, they are headed to the shipyard."

One of the men punched in a number in his cell phone. He spoke in Hungarian to the person on the other end.

"OK, we have people on the ground, they are covering the east and west entrances to the yard. You can't get in or out any other way unless you swim."

***

Marie's eyes feel like sandpaper as she struggles to open them. She realizes her hands are handcuffed behind her back, and she is tied with a scratchy rope to a chair. She looks around the cell-like room. She is alone, for now. She hears a click like a microphone loudspeaker.

"Welcome Marie Vuillard, or should I call you Ms. Beethoven." She hears several people laughing in the background.

"This will be your home for as long as you live which, I hope will not be long. We want the letters and some information. You will give it to us."

Marie doesn't speak, she's not sure if she can. Her throat is so dry she can hardly swallow.

"Water, water."

She manages to squeak out the word.

"Ah, you need water, *hmm*, well, I need answers. Perhaps we can help each other. Yes?"

"What... do... you... want... to... know?"

"That's better. Where are the letters, where is the last letter?"

Marie is cursing them inside her head. She hopes Viktor called Braun even though she's not sure if would care. *He cares, you just need a chance to talk*. Maire hears the piano's voice trying to soothe her. She closes her eyes and concentrates on the voice, wishing all this was just a bad dream.

"HEY!"

Marie hears the man shouting over the loudspeaker, it is so loud she cries out.

"OK! OK, please, I don't feel well."

"The letters, tell me what I want, or you will feel real pain."

"I don't have the letters." In truth, she did not. She knows where they are, but that's not what he asked.

"I don't know about the last letter."

"Where are the letters, Marie? Tell me now, or I will send Imre in and he will make you tell me."

Marie wanted to stall for time. Surely Viktor and Braun would come for her. She prayed they would come. She didn't have to pretend to be upset so she used that to her advantage. She cried as she spoke.

"What makes you think I have them. You think they trust me? You're wrong, they torture me…" She sobbed and let her voice trail off.

Torture, the word was an apt enough metaphor, close to the truth, after all seeing Braun and Hanna was torture. Marie was doing her best to stall and to get more information. She hears a heavy door behind her open then footsteps.

"This is Imre, he wants to know more."

Imre unties Marie's hands and pushes her hands in her lap. He drags a small wooden desk from across the room and pushes it in front of her.

"Hands, up here," he says as he pounds his fist on the desk.

"No, no, I told you all I know, let me go!"

Marie hears more than one person laughing over the loudspeaker.

Imre grabs Marie's right hand.

"No, not my hands, please!"

"Then talk or you will never play the piano again."

"I don't have the letters, but I, I know where they keep them. I'll tell you."

Marie's thoughts were spinning, where could she say the letters were? She could not tell the truth; she didn't want to lead them to poor Ivan in Megyer, and she did not want to lead them to Braun. Think Marie! Apparently, she was taking too long to think. Imre's anvil-like hand slammed down on hers, and she winced with pain. She was sure he broke at least two of her fingers. Panic rose in her and the words spat out of her mouth before she could stop them.

"A small village, a farm outside Budapest."

"What village, the name please."

Marie hated herself for telling them, but she knew it would take at least two hours to reach Megyer. If she was lucky, Viktor and Braun would find her by them. It was the best of the options. She was in great pain; her hand was swelling up like a balloon in front of her eyes and turning black. She could not catch her breath. She thought surely, she would pass out any minute. Instead, she threw up on Imre's shoes.

Imre, slapped Marie across the face and swore at her in Hungarian. More laughing over the loudspeaker. Her face stung, and she felt herself losing consciousness, everything turned to black.

The sting of freezing cold water snapped Marie back into consciousness. She was still here; this terror was still happening to her. Her heart sank, she sobbed uncontrollably.

"You were telling us the name of the village before you so rudely fell asleep."

Marie dreaded saying it, but she had no choice.

"An M, it begins with an M, I, I can't remember…"

Irme kicked Marie in the leg, and she let out a blood curdling scream. Unbeknownst to her, he had a razor blade sticking out from the toe of his shoe. Blood everywhere. Marie felt her pant leg getting wet, her skin sticking to the fabric as the blood drained out of her.

She had no more fight in her. She passed out and prayed to God, if this was her last moment on earth, he would take her now, have mercy on her and take her quickly.

Chapter Fourteen

Hear me Marie, follow the sound of my voice. You will not be forsaken; you will not be lost. I am here, we are here. Rest, let your mind settle, listen to my music. He will come for you, and you shall live. You are the keeper in this time, love will prevail. Hold on, don't let go!

Marie is in pain and there is something icy under her nose. She manages to open her eyes to see Braun, Hanna, and Viktor at her bedside. The icy feeling is the oxygen tube just inside her nostrils. She lifts her hand, which is bandaged and heavy, to Braun. He gently puts her hand on her chest and holds her arm.

"My love, I am here."

Marie looks into his eyes and starts to weep. She drifts out of consciousness in a foggy whirl of clouds and stars, she tries to speak, but cannot hear her own voice. Silence. A sting like fire in her arm. Her heartbeat steadies and she is warm and at ease. She is walking in a place she has been, the museum perhaps, she can't tell yet. She is at the Broadwood, playing to her heart's content. The room dissolves into a beautiful meadow, surrounded by a forest with birds chirping, and a soft breeze lilting around her. She hears the piano speak to her again.

You must know he loved you, though you never met. He loved her; she was his true love. His genius was not conceivable to most of the people around him, but you should understand, I believe you understand. You were born to move the world forward, my dear Marie, you must move forward, you must keep his secrets. The world made music a cruel mistress to him, to me, and to her. He longed for an ordinary life, marriage, and children. We both know it could never have been.

Free yourself now, I beg you, from the ills of your past, for that is why you were born. Fulfill his wish in your life, his last wish to see his ancestors live a normal life.

Begin again with Braun. I am a jealous lover Marie, I wanted you for my own as I wanted her. But I need to be at peace now, in silence. For there is not one note, or chord I have not sounded, I have destroyed all that I can in the name of revenge and lust. Silence me, now Marie, play me, promise me you will keep our secrets and promise you will live the life you were fated to. Do this and his magic, his enduring love will be yours. You will never feel alone again, you will have whatever your heart desires, all that one lifetime can offer.

Bless you Marie, bless you, may God keep you.

Marie is thrashing in her bed. Her IV slipped out, causing the alarm bell on the machine go off. She hears the piercing sound, a constant, urgent ring in her dreams. She runs toward it, stumbling on cobblestone streets, slipping on the slick slate stairs. She bangs her fists on the heavy wood door, "Open please, let me in!" she hears herself screaming. Silence. She feels the whooshing of petticoats under her dress, hears the slight tap, tap, of her satin shoes on the polished marble floor. Tapestries with deep crimson borders and gilded thread cover the immense walls from floor to ceiling, fireplaces so big you could stand in them, and she hears the far-off echo of a harpsicord coming from somewhere nearby.

Marie walks through room after room luxuriously appointed with gold leaf furniture, cushions, rugs, paintings, gold tea sets, and velvet swirling in a vortex around her, she is dizzy and weak. Suddenly, it stops.

Now comfortably seated on a blue velvet settee, Marie watches a man and woman with their backs to her sitting on a bench in front of a piano. The man and woman are laughing and caressing, singing and they kiss passionately. Marie hears the piano and yet, neither the hands of the woman or the man are on the keys. She gets up and walks toward them. As she gets closer, she recognizes them, Beethoven, and Evangeline. It cannot be! The woman turns to her, but looks through her as if she is a ghost. Her face, it is Evangeline and yet it is not. Her features are so similar, her manner so much like Evangeline's, but Marie can see it is not in fact, her. Beethoven is fiercely handsome and rugged. He stands and Marie notices his stature is shorter than she imagined and yet, he seems to fill the space in the room, his sheer presence is formidable, sexy, and commanding. The woman leans into him and whispers in his ear. He laughs and begins to undo the buttons on the back of her dress. Marie walks very close to them, but they do not acknowledge her.

*He is revealing himself and her to you. Believe,
Marie!*

Marie hears the familiar voice of the piano. She walks to
the keys, lightly touches them, and hears the piano moan.
She jumps back. She gingerly touches them again and
hears the same moan.

Music fills her head; her eyes are closed, and she is
moving to the music. Now when she opens her eyes again,
she sees Beethoven alone at the Broadwood. He is
composing. Like watching a woman give birth it is
magical, dangerous, and exhilarating. Beethoven is
humming, counting in German, and talking to the piano.
He abruptly gets up and smashes his hand on the side of
the piano. The air in the room is thin, Marie feels as if a
giant elastic band has been stretched back, the violent
release imminent. She looks for a way out. Beethoven is
pacing, yelling in German, his fists punching the air.
Silence. Blackness, then music.

Beethoven is standing at the piano, listening. Soft,
slow, adagio, then glissando, the notes slide from one to
the other silently asking permission to proceed, a bit
louder, but still so soft. He is conducting now his hands
making a slow sweep right then left, up and down, he
moves back to the keys and speaks in German to the piano.
All seems well again, there are no marks on the piano
where he smashed his fist. Marie's stomach is turning. She
knows she should leave, but she desires nothing more than
to stay.

"Marie, Marie, can you hear me?"

Marie hears her name and feels a hot sting on her arm. She is awake, the needle in her arm brings her back to the present. *What just happened?* The nurse, Braun they are looking down at her in her hospital bed, their faces are strained and flushed.

"Braun, what is it, what's wrong?"

"We almost lost you, Marie." He falls into the chair beside her bed. She wants to tell him she was not lost she had moved backward in time; she was with Beethoven and the Immortal Beloved, she saw them! The mood in room is tense, Marie decides to let Braun settle. She scared him, she didn't mean to, but he is visibly shaken.

"It's all right my love, it's all right."

Marie tries to comfort him, her voice low and full.

Braun comes close to her and whispers, "You are OK, you will be OK. I love you, nothing else matters."

She lets him hold her as he weeps. A nurse breaks the silence in the room and shoos everyone out. Braun refuses to leave and speaks to the nurse in Hungarian. He is allowed to stay. The nurse is fidgeting with Marie's IV and pushing buttons on the monitors surrounding her. Marie notices Braun's face is bruised, he has a cut on his lip and a bandage on his hand.

"Braun, you're hurt."

"No, I am fine, just scratches. And, you are fine, my love. We found you in time. You will be all right. The doctor says your hand will heal and you will play again. Don't worry."

"Please tell me they are all in jail."

Braun didn't respond right away. Marie could see he was hiding something. Then it dawned on her; he kissed Hanna. Hanna, why was she here?

"The people who survived our raid are in jail."

Marie knew that meant some of the HHPS were dead. She could not feel sad about that fact, not right now.

"Braun, I have to know. Are you and Hanna having an affair?"

"Meine Liebe, I know you saw us, and I need to explain. I won't lie to you, not now, not ever. Hanna and I share a long past. I went to her to ask for the last letter which she's had for many years. The letter is important to her, but she understood, it belongs to you. She kissed me goodbye, she now knows how much I love you, that she and I will never be again. That is the truth."

Whether it is because of all she had endured, all she had learned about herself these last few months, or just the morphine filling her veins, Marie did not argue with Braun, she didn't want to. She wanted to accept he loved her, plain and simple. She did not want anything to come between them ever again. She smiled and took his hand.

Viktor and Hanna gingerly enter Marie's room. Marie motioned for them to come in.

"My little friend, I am so glad you are OK." Viktor kissed her hand as tears welled in his eyes.

"Viktor, you are my friend, my true friend. Thank you for everything."

"Braun, Viktor, could you give Hanna and I a moment alone?"

Hanna came close to Marie, wiping tears from her eyes.

"Marie, please forgive me. I am not the monster you may think. I know how Braun feels about you and you must understand how I feel about him. He and I share a past, a family, a country. We love each other, but not as he loves you. He is my brother, my comrade, and my best friend. I hope you and I can be friends, too. Please marry him, do not let my foolishness stop you, I really could not bear it."

"Well, he has not asked me to marry him, but I understand what you are saying. I want to believe you, and I want us to be friends. I may need a little time to warm up to your relationship with him, I hope you understand."

"Take your time, Marie. I want nothing but happiness for you both, I swear it, you will see."

***

Now that visiting hours are over, the hospital is quiet again. Marie convinced Braun to go home and get some rest. In truth, she needed rest too, and she wanted to be alone. Marie knows there are conversations she and Braun must have, but for now, healing comes first.

Thankfully, her private room has a large window. Marie can see the moon and stars beginning to show themselves as evening envelopes Budapest. Unlike American hospitals, the window is not permanently locked, and the nurses think fresh air is good for their patients. Marie breathes deeply, feeling grateful to be alive and to be alone. She drifts off to sleep easily.

Once again, Marie is walking through gilded rooms. She hears people talking and is eager to get to them. As she enters the piano room, Beethoven and the woman, The Immortal Beloved are arguing. She is begging him to take her hand.

"Please, I care not who sees, I am yours, I want to look at my hand and be reminded of you, our love which is as enduring as this gold."

"No! I won't risk it. You will not be shunned as I have had to endure; you know not what torture it is. I gave it to you in hopes you would wear it on a chain at your breast or keep it safe in your jewel box. I cannot allow you to risk ridicule. You must understand."

The woman sobs and falls to her knees on the floor, her light blue satin gown makes a river of light around her. Beethoven kneels in front of her. They exchange more tender words, but Marie cannot make out what they are saying. Marie moves closer to them.

Beethoven speaks in a low voice, but Marie can hear him.

"Our doomed fate is that we cannot be ordinary, my love. My love for you will endure until the end of time. This ring is, but a mere token, a symbol. I cannot bear to think what your father would do to you if he saw it."

"Soon you will be gone from me, I want to hold onto everything you have given me, clutch it to my heart. Oh, Ludwig, I am at your mercy, always. You are right of course. He watches me, he knows I long for you. I shall long for you always, that is my torture in this life."

Beethoven taps the piano with his fist.

"This madman, my liege, my muse, he knows of our hearts as no other. I will put this in his belly. When I am gone, take it, hide it, keep it until you are free. Then promise me you will wear it, give it to our child."

Marie is standing a few feet from the piano. She watches as Beethoven bends in close under the lid places the ring somewhere in the piano. He helps his lover to her feet and kisses her as he escorts her out of the piano room.

When Beethoven returns, he walks very close to where Marie is standing and stares at her, not through her, but directly at her. Marie gasps and begins to speak. She can feel her lips moving, she feels her hand on her stomach as she pauses to breathe, but she cannot hear anything. Beethoven slowly turns away from her. Blackness.

Chapter Fifteen

The fireplace in Braun's living room fills the space with a warm glow and soothing warmth. It's been ten days since Marie was released from the hospital.

"Meine Liebe, you look positively radiant today."

"I feel like myself again. Thank you for taking me here, for taking care of me."

"No thanks needed; I will always take care of you. I'm glad you are feeling well enough to have dinner at Hanna's this evening, I know she is looking forward to our visit."

"I'm well enough, I know it's important for us to go. Although, I would like to visit Hans and Sarah at the rehab hospital, maybe, we can go tomorrow?"

"Yes, definitely, let's plan on it."

***

Marie is holding Braun's hand as they take the elevator to the nineth floor, Hanna's apartment. Braun pushes a button on the elevator panel, and it comes to a halt.

"Braun, what are you doing? We aren't at the nineth floor yet."

"I want you to know, I love no other, I never have. The fact that you trust me enough to be here, makes me

149

love you even more. Know this Meine Liebe, you are my one true love."

Marie and Braun kiss passionately in the elevator. The door chime sounds as the elevator has not moved in over fifteen minutes. They laugh as Braun pushes "9," and the elevator continues upward.

"Welcome, you two, thank you for coming."

Marie hands Hanna a bouquet of flowers.

"Red Tulips, the national flower of Hungary. Marie, thank you, this means so much, a symbol of friendship I hope."

"I have come to love this country, and I know how much you love it too, Hanna."

"Sit please, let me pour you a drink."

Hanna pours wine and the three of them sit in the small living room. Marie is next to Braun on the couch and Hanna is in a chair across from them. The conversation is easy, easier than Marie thought it would be.

At the dinner table, the talk inevitably turns to the HHPS and the letters. Sarah has been in rehab, her vocal cords are damaged, but she is learning to speak again with therapy. The lawsuits against Braun's family have been dropped, for now.

"Hanna, if you don't mind telling me, how did you come upon the last letter, and when?"

"Ah, yes, it's a good question Marie and you should know the answer. In fact, it is one of the reasons I invited you here. "

Settling themselves in the living room, Brandy in hand, Marie was anxious. She wanted to learn about the last letter, she needed to learn about it. But it represented an ending. She had begun to feel a closeness to her famous ancestor; she had begun to share his melancholy. Maybe, it was because she saw them together in her dreams, dreams she has not yet shared with Braun. She saw him put a ring inside the Broadwood, and she could not wait to be alone with the piano to search for it. Most likely, it was long gone. Another piano technician probably found it decades ago. Yet, she never read anything about it in their diaries or in the historical accounts of his life. She needed to find out for herself. After all, it was meant for her to find. Marie could not help, but shiver. She had come to fully accept her family lineage; she had no doubts anymore. She felt herself slipping into stillness, sleep walking through this evening. She watched Braun and Hanna, heard them talking, but she was not fully present. Now, her sole purpose for being in Budapest was to find the ring and decide what to do with the letters. She wanted to be close to the piano, the only thing in existence that knew Beethoven as well as his Immortal Beloved. She needed to know more. Her thoughts were a vortex of the past and present, she was drifting away from Hanna's living room.

"Meine Liebe, did you hear me, Marie?"

Marie snapped out of her stupor to see Braun and Hanna staring at her.

"I apologize, I seem to be lost in my own thoughts. Forgive me, what did you say Braun?"

"Hanna asked if you had talked to Viktor or Ivan recently."

151

"No, as a matter of fact I have not. Have you?"

"I spoke to Viktor last night. He fears the remaining members of the HHPS are planning another ambush. This time, it will be a bloody war, not merely a battle. He is in hiding with Ivan, he fears for his life and Ivan, too. He also fears for the three of us. We are all connected in this web of lies, whether we want to be or not."

"And where do you stand, Hanna? Will you help Braun and I, or are you considering your options?"

"Marie, that was very callous. Hanna has invited us here to talk about the letters. Of course, she is going to help us."

Silence. Marie stares at Hanna. She surprised herself with her bold, direct confrontation of Hanna, but something inside her propelled her to speak. She did not regret it.

"She is right to question me, Braun, I think you know that. When love is forbidden, a woman will search for any means of comfort, even if it comes in the form of revenge. I think Marie knows this somehow, yes?"

"I have not experienced it, but yes, I do know it. I have friends here Hanna, unlikely allies."

Braun is on his feet now, pacing. Hanna hasn't moved a muscle in her chair. Her gaze remains fixed on Marie, her hand on her wine glass. The only sound in the room is the pop and crackle of the logs in the fireplace.

"It's true, I have a lot to gain from accepting the HHPS offer. But it comes at a price I am not willing to pay. You think me cold and ruthless Marie, and maybe, I am, or at least a part of me is. But you are American. You can't

152

possibly know how deep my roots in Hungary are. You can't possibly understand how much we have sacrificed. My family, Braun's family, our blood is in the soil of this country. We owe it our lives. I think some Americans take for granted their freedom and safety, the shield your country provides. It is not so in Hungary. Braun and I are patriots first. We learned at a young age duty and country come first, even before family and certainly before the self. I would never betray my country, I could not. It is not in my bones to do so."

Marie catches Braun's gaze and notices he is fighting back tears. Her heart pounds for him, her love for him is deep. Still, something inside will not let her relent. She must not appear weak in this moment, although she is not entirely sure why it matters.

"I admire your patriotism. I know it is a deep part of Braun, too. But you don't know who I am, not really. If I am truly the descendant of Beethoven, and I feel I am, I have roots here, too. Roots that despise the shallow people who dictate societal norms, class, and rank. I want to read all the letters again, I want to decide for myself what Beethoven, what she, would have wanted. Whether or not the letters should have been kept hidden, I cannot say right now. But I am not convinced it was the right thing to do. I'm sorry, Braun, I should have told you."

Silence. Braun looks at Marie, his face sad and strained as if he had been kicked in the stomach. Hanna's face is unchanged. She is staring at Marie, her mind churning like ice in a blender.

"I'm going to make some coffee and give you two a chance to speak. I think we could all use a break in this conversation."

Braun and Marie are alone. Marie wants to run into his arms, tell him she loves him. Another part of her strongly feels the need for restraint, hesitancy. Marie remains seated on the couch.

"Do you despise me Meine Liebe, have I failed you? I feel you are turning away from me, but I don't know why. Please tell me."

"I am not turning away from you, and I don't want you to think I am, not for a moment. But something is changing inside me Braun, I cannot explain it now, and I don't want to talk about it here in Hanna's house. If you love me, trust me. Let me go to the piano, alone. Let me figure this out for myself. I am just asking for time, and of course, your trust. Can you do that for me?"

"Perhaps some coffee will help sober our thoughts."

Hanna puts a large silver tray with coffee and little desserts on the table in front of the fireplace. Braun and Marie do not speak.

"I sense something, are you two quite all right?"

Braun sits next to Marie and takes her hand.

"Yes, we are all right. But Marie needs to go to the piano, you don't mind do you Hanna?"

Marie speaks before Hanna answers.

"Thank you, Braun. I do need to go to the piano, but first, Hanna, please finish telling us how you got the last letter. Then I will leave."

"Of course, Marie. I had the letter for a long time, longer than you may know Braun, my friend. I have spent years taking care of this museum, the antique instruments are like my wards, I care deeply for them. I think that is a sentiment you and I share, Marie. Many times, I would go to the Broadwood, sit by it, play it. Yes, I would play it even though I am not supposed to. I needed to hear it; I can't explain, but it gave me comfort. Sometimes, I thought I heard the piano speak to me, maybe, not words exactly, but feelings. I felt the longing this piano had for its master, for Beethoven. It became a ritual for me to visit it. I felt guilty if I did not. One summer evening the power in the museum went out due to a storm. At that time, the doors to the exhibit rooms would automatically lock if the power went out. I ended up locked in the piano room."

"When was this Hanna, was I here or at university?"

"Ah, I was young, you were at university Braun, yes. I think I was all of twenty-one."

"So, at that time, my father and older brother ran the museum, until my father died."

"Yes, my friend, your father and Franc were here."

"I'm sure you both know the story of Zoltan, yes? Well, at that time I was consumed with his story. We found a partial diary in the desk of the piano room. It was hidden in one of the panels. The diary his grandson was in possession of began where this one left off, a good thing for us. I took the diary from the archives and read it every night. I found out Zoltan had the last letter. Why he did not give it to your great grandfather, I do not know. But he did not. Instead, he hid it in the piano. I think it was because

155

he wanted the letter to remain in the company of Beethoven, or his spirit which would most likely be with the piano. I imagine Zoltan was a romantic, this is conjecture, but I believe it."

"In the piano, where in the piano, did you find anything else?" Marie's mind was racing, *the ring, she must have found the ring, too.*

"No, I did not find anything else. The letter was in the leg of the piano. Among his many other talents, Zoltan was a master carpenter. He carefully took apart the left, front leg of the piano at the top, where the frame of the piano sits. He was able to place the letter there and replace the panel, seamlessly. To my knowledge, no restorer has ever noticed the altered panel. I had a friend at the time, who was also a master carpenter. He promised to keep the secret and agreed to help me. He was able to take the leg apart, just as Zoltan did, and we found it."

The last letter was inside the piano, Marie's heart raced. She remembered what Beethoven wrote to Thomas Broadwood, the maker of the great 1817 Broadwood after he had received it:

"I shall look upon it as an altar upon which I shall place the most beautiful offerings of my spirit to the divine Apollo…"

He's done exactly that; his most cherished possessions are inside the piano!

"Thank you, Hanna, for telling us the truth about the last letter. I hate to be rude, but I must go to the piano, now, alone."

Marie gathered her things; Braun is at her heels.

"I promise, I will be all right, I'll text you when I am finished. Stay, visit with Hanna. I will get the driver to take me to your place."

She hurriedly kissed Braun and left Hanna's place. The piano was on the same floor as Hanna's rooms. She walked the long corridor, used her keycard at the entry to the antique instruments area and headed to the Broadwood. Once inside, she locked the heavy door behind her, flipped on the light switch and the room buzzed with a loud hum. She covered her ears and waited. As it subsided, she softly spoke.

"I am here, I know your secrets, I won't betray you. Help me to understand more, he would want it, I'm sure."

The buzzing ceased. Marie went to the piano. She sat down on the floor next to the left, front leg. Marie talked to the piano, she no longer cared if it was crazy, she knew in her soul she was where she was meant to be, this exact moment, and in Hungary. Looking at the piano leg, she spoke aloud.

"You can hardly tell, Zoltan was a master, a good soul too."

She traced the barely visible seal around the support box where Zoltan hid the letter.

"Zoltan must have heard you speak, too, and he was true to you and to him."

Marie laid under the piano, looking for any anomaly that would lead her to the ring.

"He came to me; you already know that. He showed her to me, I saw them together. So tragic and beautiful. She looks just like my aunt Evangeline, I thought at first it was

157

her. And she looks a little like me. I cannot deny what I saw, I cannot pretend I don't know in my soul, she is my ancestor, too. I am at your command my dear friend, you know that by now, don't you?"

Marie waited for a reply, but none came.

"Beethoven said he hid the ring in your belly. Please help me find it."

Marie came out from underneath the piano and lifted the lid, placed the wood support in in place and slowly ran her across the strings, the pins, and in each niche and the places where the original Broadwood craftsmen like Mr. Murray, signed their names. Priceless history, and untold stories, live in this piano. *They must be set free,* Marie thought.

"Follow me."

Marie heard the voice again which was deep and warm from inside the piano. She waited; her eyes peeled for any movement. The room is silent except for the soft, click, click, of the air temperature regulator. Marie closes her eyes as the sound of a strong, beautiful, minor A fills the room. The strings vibrate as the sound trails off. She gently touches the vibrating strings and follows them to the top where it wraps around the pin. She sees something wedged between a pin and the hammer. She uses her pointer finger to touch it and it flies out from the piano and lands on her chest. She can hardly breathe, *the ring!*

Marie's hand is shaking, the small gold ring, a delicate piece of forgotten history, his history, and now hers, feels electrically charged in her hand. *She must have been so small*, Marie thought, the tiny ring does not fit her. She looks at the inside, an inscription reads:

Ever thine, LVB, 1826.

Marie wipes a tear from her eyes, the words, "Ever thine" the same words he wrote in one of his last letters to his lover. "Ever thine, ever mine, ever ours."

"Thank you, thank you for trusting me, my friend. You will always have a piece of my heart."

The piano doesn't respond, but Marie feels its presence. The ring glides easily on her pinky and Marie smiles. The gravity of what just happened starts to sink in and she sits on the floor next to her confidant and friend. The piano room feels like home now, a place she doesn't want to leave. The Broadwood comforts her, the kinship they have formed feels like a giant puzzle piece, put in exactly the right place, filling a vacant hole in the picture of her life. Braun, he is another piece of her life she desperately needs. Marie loves him, she knows she tests his love, but this situation is extraordinary, surely, he understands.

Marie knows Braun is waiting for her, and she will have to explain about the dream, the ring, and how she feels so deeply connected to Beethoven now, her ancestor. There is no question in her mind, she will do whatever it takes to protect him and his love. They wished for their relationship to remain secret, of that, she is sure.

"There are ways to protect him and still reveal their love to the world. But I know, you and he would prefer it remains secret. I understand why it was the prudent thing to do in his time, but now... still, I won't betray him or you, my dear friend. I understand my duty, and I understand why it must be me who ensures the secret remains hidden. I'm grateful I have the ring which I'd like to keep. I hope that's all right."

Marie hears the faint reply. *"It is yours."*

She feels the pain the Broadwood feels. He has lived with the ring and these secrets for so long, they have become part of him, his legacy, a legacy no one will know. Removing the ring is akin to removing a piece of his heart, a piece he knows he cannot keep. No one will weep for the Broadwood, or come to understand the magic he possessed, the true friendship he gave even in the face of punishment from the master himself. So many years, centuries of waiting, grief, anger locked inside his soul, his body an obligatory vessel for the secrets of history. Did they feel like a burden? Or like a tumor, growing, burgeoning out of the borders of what he could tolerate? Did he long for the day they were removed when he could be free? Marie knew the answer.

The last letter and the ring. They were a part of him, placed inside his bones. The Keeper, that's what the note she received in the library called her, but the Broadwood was the real Keeper, and he was loyal accepting his fate without remorse. They gave him no choice. Marie had no doubt the piano loved his master and yet, she could not help but feel sad for the extraordinary life the piano had, and for the horrific pain it witnessed and endured.

The Broadwood was a confidant in the truest sense of the word. He came alive under Beethoven's hands; he gave unconditional love and duty to his master. Marie knew what historians said about Beethoven, he was prone to mad fits of rage. He took out his anger at the world on the Broadwood. He would smash his fists on its sides, he would slam the lid down without regard for the soul living inside, the soul powerless to fight back. Beethoven often wrote how the Broadwood was his life's companion in a world which routinely shunned him and mocked him. He called the piano a "madman" no doubt referring to himself as well as the utterly abiding piano who was his captive.

I would have been ordinary wood, pieces of ivory, and wire without him. Without Beethoven I would have been just another piano bearing the Broadwood name tossed aside as greater, more advanced instruments were made. He gave me a life, he gave me meaning, a place in history. His was a sad tale of loss, so much loss. How could he have borne it alone? His Immortal Beloved, she and he had pitiful few stolen moments together, so few in fact, most people would not have lasted such a test. But their love was timeless, and it lasted beyond his death, of that, I am sure.

Shall I tell you another secret? I was put on display in the late 1800s as the museum tried in vain to raise money for renovation. I was trotted out and put on show as one of the more priceless objects the museum owned. To be owned, the word enrages me even now. No one owns me. Since his death, I am an orphan. The day was horrible, raining like the tears he would have shed had he known what they did to me. Many came, but she was there. I sat indignant as throngs of onlookers walked by me, pointed at me, whispering, laughing. She waited until she and I were alone in the room. She came as close as possible pushing herself against the rope which separated me from her. She spoke in German.

"Menine andere wahre Leibe." My other true love, this is what she said. And then she spoke his words, the words he wrote to her which she deemed to grace on me.

"Ever thine, ever yours, ever ours." I could not bear it. She was shooed away before I could speak, I was heartbroken, but I managed to call out to her, "My love" as she walked away. I never saw her again.

And now, I am far too old Marie, my duty is all but done. You have all you need to keep the secret safe, except for one key secret. This final step you must do Marie, it is the final test of your love for him. I can finally be at rest if you do this one last act of love and selflessness, you must Marie.

Marie listened intently to the piano; his pain was palatable. What was the last step?

"Of course, I will do anything, tell me."

Marie heard a knock. Braun, he must have gotten tired of waiting for her. Marie had no idea how long she had been with the piano. She hesitated, she did not want this intrusion, but she thought better about not letting him in and opened the door.

"Marie, I'm sorry to disturb you, but something has happened."

"It's OK, what happened?"

"I think you better come with me; this can't wait."

Marie twisted Beethoven's ring on her pinky and silently said goodbye for now, to the piano.

Chapter Sixteen

The skin on Braun's face was tight, his eyes never left the road as they drove outside the city on winding, country roads. Marie thought at first, they were headed to Megyer, but she did not recognize the names of the towns they passed along the way. She knew Braun must be upset with her for leaving Hanna's place so abruptly, for spending so much time with the piano and not telling him why. Should she tell him now? She fidgeted with her scarf and touched the pinky ring again. *Now is as good a time as any*, she thought.

"Braun, I know you are a little upset with me, but I have something to tell you."

Braun did not speak right away, he took in a deep breath and remained silent for a moment longer.

"I'm not upset with you, Meine Liebe. I am fearful of what we learn in this meeting, and I am concerned about your safety. Whatever secrets you have from me, I don't care. I love you, that will not change."

"I do have something to tell you, but it's not a secret, I just needed more time with the piano to figure it all out. I think I have now, and I need to tell you, if you want to listen."

Braun reached for her hand and gently placed it on his leg. "Of course, please."

"It may sound odd to you, but I can hear the piano speak. It has been communicating with me since I got here. At first, I wasn't sure if it was just my excitement about being here, my amazing good fortune at having the chance to play such an important historical instrument. But I soon realized, it was more than that. The piano does communicate with me."

Marie waited; did he think she was crazy? She started to speak, but he interrupted her.

"Marie, my sweet Marie, I understand more than you know. This may sound strange to you, but I think the piano hates me. I know it has spoken to Zoltan, even Hanna, but never me. I don't know why, but he doesn't like me near him. I feel certain of it in my bones."

Marie started to laugh and caught herself. Braun wasn't so quick to see humor in situations, maybe, it was his Hungarian military upbringing, but Marie learned to explain herself, so Braun didn't think she was being rude.

"I'm only laughing because you are exactly right. He told me so. He is jealous of you, my love. He sees me as a sort of reincarnated Immortal Beloved, he wishes he were human. Does that make sense?"

Braun smiled.

"It makes perfect sense. So, what do you want to tell me?"

"When I was in the hospital, I had dreams, dreams that were so real. I was in a very ornate house and the piano was there and... Beethoven, too. I saw him and the Immortal Beloved. I saw him kiss her, heard what they said to each other and later, I witnessed something extraordinary."

"More extraordinary than hearing them speak? That is something."

"Beethoven gave her a ring. He told her to wear it on a chain around her neck or to keep in her jewelry box, but not to wear it on her finger. She disobeyed him and they got into an argument. She begged him to let her wear it. It seemed like she knew he was going to die soon. She said she wanted to keep anything that reminded her of him, close to her. She was weeping, it was so sad."

"This is incredible, is there more?"

"Yes. He consoled her and they spoke to each other with such love, such compassion. I've never witnessed such pure emotion before. I was weeping, too. He put the ring inside the piano and told her to retrieve it after he was gone and to give it to their child. As far as I know, it would have been impossible for her to get anywhere near the piano after his death. After all, no one knew how close they were and I'm sure the Broadwood was well guarded, even in the late 1800s."

"You're right, it was. No one except the museum director and curator would have access to it. Only a handful of people were allowed near it. Of course, it was given to Liszt at Beethoven's request right after his death. Who knows how many people he had at his home? Although, it is said he never played it."

"Well, I wondered the same which is why I had to go the piano and see for myself if it was there. After Hanna told me about the last letter, I knew the ring was still in the piano. It's hard to believe no one found it. The piano restorers would have been all over the piano and many took it apart. I was shocked, but Braun, it was there."

Marie held up her pinky finger to show Braun the ring.

"My God, Marie!"

"It's unfathomable I know, but here it is. The piano led me to it. I knew I had to speak to him, to communicate my heart and let him speak to me. Braun, he is a sad, tormented soul. He needs to be free, to be silent. I feel so deeply connected to him now. I have to set him free."

"How will you do that, Meine Liebe?"

"I've decided the letters must be kept hidden. This is so much bigger than me, than my one life, it is Beethoven's life, her life, and all his ancestors who came after. Beethoven and the Immortal Beloved struggled to keep some semblance of peace and normalcy to their lives. The only way they could achieve that was to keep their love secret. I understand now. In our time, it would not be such a scandal, but it would change what we know about Beethoven. It would be another news story, people would talk. It would be like opening the wound they desperately tried to heal. It was their life outside of music, something he cherished. He was aware of what society thought of him and the persona they invented for him; the mad maestro who never married because he was too crazy, too violent.

It's like what they did to Marilyn, they created the persona of Marilyn Monroe to sell movie tickets and magazines, but that person was an illusion it was not Norma Jean. Beethoven was not the illusion they created either. To expose their secret would be a betrayal to the

166

truth. People will create more false stories about them to suit their own fantasies. I cannot do it; I won't do it."

"But if the world knew the truth, their truth, it would stop the falsehoods? It might put things right."

Marie was silent. She had not expected Braun to play devil's advocate. Maybe, she didn't know him as well as, she thought. Her insides were churning, she felt very protective of Beethoven now. She knew she had to be careful. After all, Braun had his own stakes in this. Marie noticed Braun had pulled off the road onto a dirt road by a meadow. A mild sense of alarm rose in her. She had to keep herself in check. If Braun set out to betray her here on this lonely country road, she had no way to stop him. She checked her breathing, slowly inhaled, and exhaled to keep herself calm. She decided to get him talking, to make him believe she agreed with him.

"Well, you might be right. But how would we go about doing that? The story would have to be told by people we trust."

"I could make sure of that. We have friends all over Budapest in every field you can imagine."

Marie remained silent. The longer this rouse went on, the more her insides were screaming for her to run.

"Marie, you must listen to me. I am not the man you think I am. I am a patriot as Hanna said, yes, but I am also just a man, a man in love. I told you from the start this was your decision, and I stand by that. Whatever you choose to do, it must be because you believe with all your heart. I will help you no matter what. You don't trust me, I know this. The only thing that matters is if you trust yourself. Do you want to tell the story, or do you want to keep the secret? It's as simple as that, Meine Liebe."

Marie had no words. How could he know her so well? Doubting him came easily, as if it was hard-wired into her brain, but every time she thought less of him, he surprised her. She wanted to trust Braun and if he is all he seems to be, slowly, but surely, she would break the old rules of her past. He was worth it.

"I don't want to be with a woman who would sacrifice her own beliefs to do what she thinks I want her to do or to appease me as if I were a child. I'm sorry to be so direct, but you know me well enough, and you know I am not a pliable man. I know who I am, and I know what I want. The question is, what do you want?"

"Braun, I'm sorry. You can see through me like glass, that's for sure. No, I do not want the story revealed. I want their secret to remain a secret for the rest of time. That's what I want."

Braun unlocked his seatbelt, then hers, and pulled Marie to him. He kissed her passionately, and she returned it. The sun was hiding behind clouds, but the air was warm. Braun went to her side of the car, opened the door, and held out his hand. She buried her head in his chest as he whispered in her ear.

"I want you now, here, I can't wait any longer."

Marie and Braun had not made love since she returned from the hospital. Braun restrained himself as he wanted to be sure Marie was healed physically and mentally. He longed for her, his body craved hers and it was all he could do to keep his hands off her. For a man with his voracious appetite for sex, the waiting was almost unbearable. Marie was just as hungry for Braun as he was for her. When she came home from the hospital, she still had nightmares about the attack. Braun was gentle and patient with her. But now her body ached for his, she wanted him inside her, her mouth on him, it was impossible to be too close to him. She needed him more than he knew. He grabbed a blanket from the backseat of the SUV, and they made love under a Wild Pear Tree.

A gentle rain softly pelted their bodies as Marie and Braun woke. Laughing, they hurried to put their clothes on and ran back to the SUV. Once inside, they held hands and for the first time in weeks, Marie felt safe again. Braun's phone was chirping with a text. They did not realize how much time had passed, but it had been over two hours since they left the SUV.

"I think we are in trouble Meine Liebe."

"Better to be in trouble together."

Braun hurriedly typed a few words in his phone and started the car. I'm sorry to have to break this wonderful mood, but we need to hurry, I'll fill you in on the way."

"You never told me where we were going."

"I don't want you to get upset Marie, but something unexpected has happened. It seems Viktor is having second thoughts about his loyalty."

"What? What do you mean?"

"Viktor is not staying with Ivan as he told Hanna, he has kidnapped him and is holding him at gunpoint at Ivan's farm. He sent a message saying if we try to retrieve the letters, he will kill him. And to make it worse, he called the HHPS and told them where the letters were."

"No, Braun, this can't be!"

"We are on our way to meet the members of die Wächter to help come up with a plan. I cannot honestly believe Viktor would want to harm Ivan; it doesn't add up."

"This is unreal. I never would have thought Viktor would betray us this way. Braun, is there something I don't know about him? Why would he do this?"

"I truly don't know Meine Liebe, but we will find out soon. We are almost there."

Braun pulled the SUV down a road barely visible through the thick, tangled forest and mud. They stopped at a cottage so run down, it looked abandoned. As they walked to the door, it opened. Marie stepped inside and a man she did not recognize was waiting behind the door. He put his finger to his lips, motioning for them to keep silent. He led them to a door, which led to a series of sealed doors underground. By the time they reached the last door, Marie was sure they were at least twenty feet underground. She hesitated, her head spinning. The underground passageways reminded her of the underground cell she was taken to by the kidnappers. Braun instinctively put his arm around her. They walked a narrow corridor to a room, well-lit and to Marie's surprise, warm and comfortable. Braun led Marie to a chair by the gas fireplace. The two women tech gurus were already busy monitoring their screens and taking notes. Three men sat at a round table talking. An older attractive woman walked toward Marie.

"Marie, I am Helga VonCzeck. We are the founding members of die Wächter. We are honored to have you here. If I may, let me fill you in."

The woman sat in chair next to Marie's. Another younger woman named Marta set down a tray with tea and a bottle of whiskey on the coffee table.

"This is a story of forbidden love, a tragic story. You may want to keep your glass full Marie. I'm not sure how much of this story your aunt shared with you, if any of it. But it's important you understand who Viktor really is."

***

Budapest, 2015

At dawn, in Ivan's small bathroom, yellow light filtered through the faded pink curtains she sewed six years ago. Evangeline Vuillard looked in the mirror at her stark white face. She had just thrown up blood for the fourth time that week. Death was coming for her; she could not stop it. No matter how much she loved Ivan, she would have to leave him and Marie, too. Her life, a life she was grateful for, was ending. She was in Budapest, the home of Ivan her lifelong love. *What better place to die?* She thought.

Ivan was out in the fields tending to a runaway sheep. Thankfully, Evangeline would have time to clean up, throw away the blood-stained towel, and make breakfast, just as she always did at seven in the morning. Ivan did not need to know how much the cancer had progressed. She would not have him see the blood-stained towel. She just needed to make it to Thursday, be well enough to get on a plane back to Boston. She would say everything she needed to say to him, she would say her goodbye in her own way; a way which meant he would not know this was the last time they would see each other.

The pills seemed to help so Evangeline took two instead of one as prescribed. It was a risky thing to do, but she was never good at following rules, why start now? The coffee was boiling in the old percolator coffee pot, and she had just tossed bacon in the hot pan when she heard a knock at the door.

"Ah, Viktor, my friend, come in. Are you hungry? I'm making breakfast. Sit."

"My dear, you are too good to that clod Ivan, he should know how lucky he is."

"He's lucky, I'm lucky, life is good my friend, and I have you. I am blessed."

Evangeline poured coffee for Viktor and bent down into the small refrigerator to get the bottle of cream. As she did, she almost fainted.

"My friend, careful. Are you all right?"

Viktor caught her and led her to a chair. He turned off the stove and poured coffee in her cup.

"Here, sit, drink this."

"Viktor, my dear sweet Viktor. He told you right? I am dying my friend. The cancer is advanced. They say only a few weeks now."

Viktor stood up from his chair and walked to the open kitchen door. He stood pulling at his beard, holding back the tears welling up in his eyes.

"How can this be? No, that fool, he did not tell me. My sweet, beautiful Evangeline, I cannot bear it."

Evangeline motioned for him to sit next to her again, she put her hand on Viktor's, and they sat in silence for a long time. Evangeline was touched by Viktor's emotion. She knew he cared for her, but his reaction was so strong, so dear. She smiled thinking about the fun the three friends had for so many years. The picnics by the lake, the holidays when they drank homemade rum by the small fireplace and sang until the sun came up. She wondered how long it had been since Viktor had a love of his own. She couldn't recall him ever bringing a woman to their gatherings. Poor Viktor, she thought, he is so sweet, so kind.

"Evangeline, I must be honest with you. I promised Ivan, I would never tell you, but I am devastated by this news. I cannot let you go without telling you… I love you so much, more than you know. You see my dear friend, you are my beloved, my one true love. I arrived too late; you were already taken by my friend who is also in love with you. I could never have you, but I worshiped you all these years. You had the love of two men my sweet, you should know this."

Evangeline was sobbing, using her napkin to wipe away the tears which would not stop. She loved Viktor, but she was never in love with him. He was so kind to her, so good to her and Ivan. It made sense now why he never married. Had she unwittingly prevented him from finding happiness? It was more than she could bear.

"It's all right, no tears. I made a choice my sweet. I had one or two women, but no one came close to being you. I loved you, and I made a choice to be in your life no matter if it hurt. It was my choice my dear, mine alone."

"But how could you do that? You should have married; you should have had children. Oh, Viktor, I am so sorry, I never wanted to hurt you, my dear Viktor."

"Ah, who would want to marry me anyway? A mean old man with too much hair on his body. You gave me more than you know. I learned about love from you, how you treated Ivan, the way you put up with him and with me, our antics all these years. Life is a book we write with our own pen. I wrote mine just the way I wanted. If I could not marry you, I wanted to be with you, and I was. Dry your beautiful eyes my dear."

Ivan listened at the doorway. He needed to steel himself before he went in. He knew Viktor. He was being polite for Evangeline's sake, but inside, he most likely wanted to kill Ivan. Viktor came from the rough streets of Budapest. He was no stranger to the darkness that seeps into men's hearts when they grow up on the streets. Too much poverty, too much violence, and not enough of anything makes a man forge brick walls around his heart. Viktor was a good friend, but Ivan knew full well how his friend handled betrayal, like a wounded animal, there would be no mercy for anyone who came near. Viktor caught Ivan lurking in the doorway.

"Come in you coward. She has told me everything, and I have told her. Do what you will, I am not sorry."

Evangeline went to Ivan and leaned into him. He could tell she felt ill the way her body lay limp against his. She was light as a feather, and he felt sure she would fall to the floor if he let go of her shoulders. He knew their time together was short.

"I'm glad it is all in the open."

Ivan walked Evangeline to their bedroom and put her to bed. He sat with her as she fell asleep and promised her, he would make it right with Viktor. With his fragile heart in a million pieces like shattered glass at her side, he promised.

Viktor was on his feet at the door when Ivan returned to the kitchen.

"You should be alone with her in her last days."

"Viktor, I should have told you, I know. But what good would two broken hearted men be to her? I needed your strength my friend, your optimism from being ignorant of the impending betrayal God has wrought. I know you love her, please understand."

"I understand, and I don't understand, but what does it matter? She will leave us either way. We will weep together, then who knows what will become of us."

"Viktor, I need to show you something."

Ivan walked Viktor to the woods beyond the farmhouse. He had not fully buried the letters and the wood box sat next to his shovel.

"You know who she is, yes?"

"Yes."

"These letters are hers; they are from Beethoven to the Immortal Beloved. She wants me to bury them, to keep them for her daughter, Marie. Someday, she will come to Budapest and decide once and for all what should be done. You are still a patriot my friend, yes?"

"Yes, but what does it matter?"

"I need your help. You need to know about these letters and help fulfil her wish. If I die, and if God has any mercy I will follow her soon, but who will protect her legacy, the legacy of the maestro of Hungary? Will you promise me Viktor, you will protect them, you will make sure Marie gets them if I am gone?"

"I promise my friend, but you have given me a burden I do not want. Without Evangeline in my life, I have no reason to be here. You and I were like two bees buzzing around the sweetest flower in the garden. When she is gone, what is left?"

"Please Viktor, she trusted you too, she wanted me to tell you about the letters. You cannot betray her, do this for her, not for me. I beg you."

"Then you have my word, the word of a broken man."

Viktor left Ivan's farm and did not return. Months passed, but he ignored Ivan's calls and letters. He piled up the letters and placed them in the fireplace grate. He spent the winter alone, staring at the fire. His heart was shattered his will to live waning. Viktor was betrayed, a raw feeling he knew well since childhood; old wounds, easily ripped open. He would honor Ivan's request to keep the letters safe, but he had not decided yet what defined *safe*. He would look out for himself now, a lonely, bitter man whose only lifeline to goodness and love, gone. He began thinking about revenge.

Chapter Seventeen

Marie's heart is breaking in two, but she is too far into this now to back off. *More secrets*, she thought, *why so many secrets Evangeline? Didn't you trust me, at all?*

"Marie, I can only imagine how hard this history is for you to hear. But I know Ivan. He mentored me as a fledging student in the academy and then as a struggling young cop trying to climb the ranks of the old guard. Most of the men in the force wanted nothing to do with me. I know he is honest. It's worth everything in the world to help him. I'll risk my life to see this made right, I promise you."

"I trust Ivan, too Helga. But what confuses me is Viktor. If he loved Evangeline, the way you describe, he would keep his promise and make sure I get the letters. I just don't understand."

Braun spoke in a low monotone, like a person possessed and resigned.

"Maybe, he snapped, as men often do after a life filled with heartache."

Marie looked at Braun as he spoke, *a life of heartache*, was he alluding to himself, how would he know this? Why would he say this?

"We believe Viktor has snapped. There is something else. We found evidence which suggests Viktor was involved in your kidnapping, Marie. He was there when you were trying to get a taxi to the airport, yes?"

"Now that you say it, yes, he was and it surprised me at the time, too."

"But he called me to tell me they had Marie, why would he do that if he was in on it?"

"His comrades betrayed him. Viktor thought he was there to talk Marie into giving the letters to the HHPS. They convinced him no one would get hurt. So, Vicktor swore he could change Marie's mind. When she left the museum and was upset with you Braun, it seemed like perfect timing, she was at a weak point. But Viktor's comrades merely used him, it was the easiest way to get to you, Marie. They followed him and when you left the table for the bathroom, they made their move. They had no intention of letting Viktor play it out his way."

"So now Viktor is trying to make it right with the HHPS, show them he is loyal, by threatening Ivan. This is horrible."

"More than that, it is dangerous, Marie. Viktor is desperate, we cannot trust him. The HHPS must have something on Viktor they are using as a threat. We must assume he is capable of murder, Ivan's life in danger, as is yours."

"How can we help you?"

"If you help us, both of you are putting your lives in danger, but this is an extraordinary opportunity to capture all the members of the HHPS in one place. Essentially, we need to use you as the bait."

Braun did not hesitate. "No. Never."

Marie swallowed hard. She knew full well what the HHPS were capable of. Was she brave enough? She shivered at the question. She could be hurt again, or killed, and what would she do if she saw Braun being tortured, and she was powerless to help him? This thought made her hesitate. She could not say yes, not yet.

"I need to know the entire plan. Can you give us reasonable assurances that Braun and I will not be alone? Can you promise you will have plenty of back up?"

"Yes, let me explain. Our plan is for you to call Viktor. Plead with him to let you go to Ivan's house. Lie to him and tell him you are not sure you want the letters to remain hidden. You must give the greatest performance of any actor alive, Marie. Only you know how to make him trust you. Whatever confidences you shared with him; you must use them to get him to believe you want the HHPS to have the letters. You want nothing more than for you, Viktor, and Ivan to be safe.

"When you are inside, we will surround the cottage. We already have air surveillance via drones and can clearly see where the lookouts for the HHPS are hiding. We will take them out, get into the house and protect you. There is a good chance Viktor will die trying to escape or because he tries to harm you or Ivan. Can you do this?"

"I will not allow Marie to go in there alone."

"I doubt Viktor will believe you are on his side Braun, the side of the HHPS. You cannot go in with Marie, it's that simple. You will be part of the SWAT team if you wish, but our mission is to protect Marie and retrieve the letters. The protection we can offer you is limited."

"I'm not worried about protection for myself. I've faced danger before as you know, and I will do anything to protect Marie."

"Wait, please. I need to think about this; may I have a few minutes?"

"Marie, we have only a little time, but I understand. A few minutes. I'll take you to my study, you can be alone there if you wish. We can give you is fifteen minutes at most. We need to move quickly."

Marie followed Helga to a small study. The room is windowless, but quiet, bookshelves filled with novels and books on history, even the small plant on the desk made Marie feel more at ease, *some normalcy in a crazy situation.* Braun followed and Marie did not protest.

"You know I will be close to you at all times. I won't let them harm you."

"But we can't control this situation as much as we'd all like to think we can. I have to accept I may not make it out alive, you either Braun. I wish there was some way to know what Viktor is really thinking. Do you think there is a chance he will help us?"

"If there is, it's a small one. You don't have to do this Marie. We will figure out another way, please, Marie, I can't lose you. If you were to ask me, I would tell you I don't want you to do it. That's the truth. If I can't be there, right by your side the whole time, I don't want you to do it."

Marie heard Braun but she was lost in her own thoughts. She stood by the bookshelves, twisting Beethoven's ring wondering what he would say if he knew about all this. So many lives in peril to keep his secret, and it's not the first time. History is being written, whether the story remains hidden or not, people will suffer and likely die.

Love, it's all happening because of love. Even the poor Broadwood has suffered and suffers still. Marie's thoughts are spinning, *I came here an empty canvas, yearning for color, for meaning. I found it and now, I could lose it all. My life began when I stepped off that plane in Budapest.* Marie is softly weeping, holding her sides. She hears the pleading of the piano.

Love is all there is, all there ever was. Love, music, passion. We all must die. If I were mortal, I would have died when Beethoven left this earth, sweet peace would be mine. But here I am. Only you can free me. Trust yourself Marie, help us all.

A forlorn voice, a last pleading breath. She had no choice; she could not live with herself if she did not try.

"Braun, if it's the last thing I do, we do, for love, then so be it. Will you help me?"

Braun took Marie in his arms and held her tightly. Marie knew the answer. Live or die, they would see this through together.

Chapter Eighteen

"We need your answer."

"Yes, we're on board."

Braun and Marie followed Helga back to the situation room. Two chairs waited for them at the table piled with surveillance equipment.

"Let's go over what you will say on your call to Viktor. First, you will call from your cell phone. The minute Viktor picks up, our team will ping his phone from yours to beam his location. We will know right away if he has moved from Ivan's farm. From here forward, with the beam tracker in place, we can follow him."

"Suppose he doesn't answer, or hangs up right away?"

"As long as he picks up, we've got him. Our people are already on the ground at the farm. We have lookouts, here, here, and here." Helga pointed to one of the large monitors and Marie and Braun could see infrared images of six people, two in each location.

"We have the advantage Marie, if you can get there quickly before members of the HHPS do, we will be able to ambush Viktor. But we know they are already on their way."

"Then it seems unlikely we will get there before they do."

"We have a small plane waiting. We will drop you and Braun at the farm. Team one, closest to the farmhouse, will rendezvous at the drop point and take Braun. You will have a flashlight and Braun's car keys on you. You will walk to the farmhouse and when you arrive, you will tell Viktor you parked down the road to avoid being seen. Again, it all hinges on you being convincing Marie."

"How much time do we have before the HHPS arrive?"

"We have inside two hours, conservatively. If we leave here now, you will be at the farmhouse in an under hour. That should leave you enough time to convince Viktor you are on his side. When he lays down his gun, we enter."

"But how will you know if I am successful?"

"You will be wearing a wireless microphone."

"No, it's too dangerous, there has to be another way."

"Braun, you know there is not. I told you both it was risky. This wire is undetectable, the latest technology. It's tiny, look." Helga showed Braun and Marie the microphone which was about the size of a pin head.

"We're OK with this, right Braun?"

Braun didn't speak, but nodded his head.

"It fits just behind one of the buttons on your jacket, Marie. There's no reason Viktor should suspect anything. But you must wear your jacket or make sure it is in the room with you at all times, remember that."

"Got it."

Braun scratched the stubble on his chin and sighed. He wasn't at all comfortable with this plan and Marie knew it. But she had to do it, what choice did she have? She could not imagine walking away now, feeling the devastating regret in her heart that would surely come every day for the rest of her life. She wouldn't be able to live with herself. And what about Braun? Would they both be able to walk away, endure whatever outcome came because they turned their backs? How could they have any kind of relationship if they both turned coward? She knew Braun better than that and she hoped he felt the same about her. They shared a commonality not easily found in a partner, the unfailing commitment to the truth. She could never walk away from such a man or from the chance to do something so important.

Helga secured the tiny microphone to the second button on Marie's jacket.

"Let's test it. Mare, please walk to the library and speak normally."

Marie did as she was instructed; Braun stayed in the situation room.

"OK, testing, one, two, three, testing. Can you hear me?"

Braun heard Marie's voice through the computer, loud and clear. The look on his face wasn't exactly relief, it was more like fear mixed with distaste. He turned away and walked to the door.

"OK, we're ready. Marie, you will call Viktor from your phone which is linked to our computer. You can call from the library if you wish or in here. Your choice. Just remember, you must appear contrite, he must believe you are on his side. Keep your voice steady, don't hesitate. The goal of this call is to get him to say yes to you coming to the farm. Got it?"

"Yes, I'm ready. I'll call from in here. You can give me the high sign if I stray off script. I'm used to playing for an audience, I'll be more focused that way."

Marie sat in a chair facing the computers and the tech team. Braun stayed near the door, Helga stood near the tech team and motioned to Marie to make the call. The clicking sound of each number could be heard as she tapped her phone. Ringing, once, twice, three times. Marie looked at Helga. Helga motioned to let it ring. Marie knew if he did not pick up, she would have to leave a damn good message. Here heart was in her throat.

Ring number four.

"Marie, what do you want?"

"Viktor, we need to talk. You have this all wrong. I'm not sure I want the letters hidden, in fact, I don't believe that's what he, Beethoven, would have wanted. I think he needs his story to be told. Will you help me?"

Silence.

Marie stared hard at the carpet, willing him to acquiesce.

"This is a surprise. How do I know you are telling me the truth? I want to trust you, but I don't trust anyone, you know that."

"Yes, I know, but even though I don't know you well, I trust what Evangeline wanted. I can't believe she wanted me to come here to protect a secret already well guarded. I think she wanted me to do the right thing. But Viktor, I want to do it my way. I don't want anyone hurt, and you have to let Ivan go. Your feud with him is not about this and you know it."

Helga mouthed the word "No" and shook her head. Marie knew she strayed off script a bit, but if the goal is to get Viktor to trust her, she had to be authentic. She did not want anyone hurt, and she was adamant about that. She had to stay close to the truth in that regard.

"And what do we do with him? Ivan will run to die Wächter the moment I turn my back."

"Not if I'm there. Let me come, I'm already on my way. We can work this out together. Who else, but us Viktor, who else could have more stake in this than us?"

Silence.

"Braun, that snake, he has a stake in it. Would you betray him?"

Marie knew this question would come. She steeled herself, her answer had to be spot on believable. No room for hesitancy.

"No, I would not. But our relationship is about more than the letters. If it's not, then I am a fool. I've been a fool before, I can live with it. He doesn't own me Viktor. This is my decision."

Braun walked out of the room and Marie felt a twinge of regret. He had to know she was just playing her part, and Marie knew Braun loved her. But all the same, her words had to sting a bit even if they were just an act.

"OK, come. Only you. I trust you Marie because Evangeline trusted you. Don't make me regret it."

Click. Viktor hung up.

A collective sigh could be heard in the situation room. Marie disconnected the call on her phone and sat back in the chair, relieved.

"Let's move, the plane is waiting."

"Wait, won't it look weird to Viktor if I arrive twenty minutes after our phone call? It's a three-hour drive."

"You told him you were already on your way, you called from the road. You had started out for the farmhouse hoping he would say yes. The flight, the walk to the farmhouse will take about an hour. It's now been twenty minutes since your call. It will have to work."

Marie did not share Helga's confidence, but she didn't protest any further. They were doing this, there was no stopping it now. The short ride to the plane was tense. Marie and Braun sat in the backseat of the SUV and held hands. She knew he trusted her, there wasn't anything they needed to say. Braun would risk his life to save hers, she was never surer of anything in her life. Marie, Braun, and Helga boarded the plane. The pilot pointed to the parachute vests stowed under the seats. Helga assured her it was just precaution, something the pilot always makes known to passengers. Marie squeezed Braun's hand, took a seat, and buckled in.

As the plane took off Marie's heart skipped a beat. No turning back. Her thoughts wandered to the Broadwood, her friend. Marie felt a deep kinship to the piano and strange as it would seem to any normal person, she wished the spirit inside it was with her now. She spoke to it silently, asking for its prayers to keep her and Braun safe. She saw the dark clouds of dusk float by, the lights of the city fading from view. She closed her eyes, taking in the sound of the air rushing outside the plane, the muted talk of the pilot and Helga in the cockpit, and the sound of Braun's breathing. The plane hit an air pocket and it felt like a car hitting a speed bump at fifty miles an hour. Marie's head hit the side wall of the plane and then quickly jerked in the other direction. Braun reached for her. The plane returned to smooth cruising and Marie let go the breath she held in her chest.

"Just a bump, everyone OK?"

The pilot's voice was calm, and Marie was grateful. Helga gave her the thumbs up, and Braun did not let go of her hand. Seconds later, the plane made a sputtering noise and an alarm sounded. Red lights on the instrument panel were blinking and the pilot was franticly pushing buttons and talking in Hungarian.

"What is it, what's happening?"

No one responded to Marie. Helga and the pilot were talking in Hungarian, Marie could tell from Helga's tone, it wasn't good.

"Something is wrong with the plane Marie; they are talking about an electrical glitch. Hold onto me."

"Parachutes!"

Helga screamed to Marie and Braun. Braun quickly pulled Marie's chute from under her seat and tossed it into her lap. He pulled his chute out and began helping Marie fasten hers. He quickly got his buckled.

"What happens now?"

Braun shouted to Helga who was having trouble with her chute.

"The rear of the plane, go to the door, now!"

Just then, the large gull wing door of the plane opened and Helga, who's chute buckle would not fasten, motioned for them to jump. Air was rushing inside as the plane jerked up and down and sputtered. Helga was holding onto her seat, frantically trying not to get sucked out of the plane.

"Jump!"

Helga screamed one last time at Braun and Marie. Braun grabbed Marie's hand and they jumped out of the plane. The air rushing around them sent them into a spiral. Braun caught Marie's hands as they flew face to face in the air, their legs outstretched behind them. This maneuver allowed them to right themselves and they opened their chutes and descended together to the ground. Helplessly, they watched as the plane dropped from the sky in a dizzying spin and crashed in an orange and red burst of flames into the ground.

Chapter Nineteen

They both hit the ground hard as neither Braun nor Marie were experienced jumpers. Landing in a clearing of trees, Braun tumbled to the left of the clearing and Marie slid on the soft ground to the right, away from Braun. When their bodies were still, the soft meadow cushioning their fall, the forest was silent. Braun was able to release himself from the parachute harness and called for Marie. Marie could hear him as if in a far-off dream. Her head was pounding, she tried to call out, but she could not catch her breath. Braun helped Marie untangle from the parachute and they sat together in the meadow, holding onto one another.

"Are you OK?"

"I think so; I got the wind knocked out of me when I hit the ground. Are you OK?"

"Yes, I landed on my knee, but otherwise, I'm OK."

"What now Braun, my God how could this have happened?"

"I'm not sure. I have no idea if the plane simply malfunctioned or if it was sabotage. Either way, we can't stay here."

"Sabotage, my God that's a frightening thought. That would mean the HHPS knows what we're up to, knows I'm on my way to see Viktor. This isn't good."

"We don't know that for sure. Could be the plane malfunctioned. Check your phone, see if anyone has contacted you."

"Oh God, yes, they have. Look."

Marie showed Braun her text messages.

"They want us to continue. I'm not sure I can. I can't believe Helga and the pilots are dead."

"They were good patriots and friends. But if the die Wächter don't suspect foul play, we have to trust them. Meine Liebe, we've come this far. What do you want to do?"

"I feel like I'm in a nightmare that won't stop. Part of me wants to run Braun. This is more than I bargained for."

"I told you I'd support whatever you decide. We are in a bad situation I know. But this is the test of us, of our commitment. We don't have much time, we either go now or quit."

"Quit, when you put it like that, I feel obligated. No, that's not right, I don't know what the hell I'm saying. Let's just do this. If the other members are in place, it's just as we've planned."

"Let's see if we can walk first, shall we?"

Braun was on his feet. He stumbled and Marie could see his knee was swollen.

"Braun, your knee. It must be fractured or badly bruised."

"I've been through worse. I can walk, I'll deal with it later. Help me hide these parachutes in the forest."

Braun and Marie quickly hid their chutes under some brush at the edge of the meadow. Marie checked her phone for directions to the farmhouse. As they walked, Marie dusted herself off and fixed her hair. Luckily, her clothes were not torn and the ordeal they had just lived through was not apparent on her body. That would have been hard to explain to Viktor.

Braun looked at the directions to the farmhouse and stopped.

"What is it, are we close?"

"Yes, that's the problem. The plane crashed in the direction of the farmhouse. We've only walked a few hundred yards and the farmhouse is just down this road. If Viktor saw the flames from the crash, he will be suspicious. He may ask you if you saw anything. We need a story."

"Oh crap, you're right. Any ideas?"

"You will tell him you saw the flames, but it seemed far away. You don't know what it was. Ask him if he knows what it was. You have to play dumb."

"Right now, I feel spectacularly dumb so that won't be a problem. Let's see, I have three lies to tell right off the bat. One, I parked my car down the road as to not attract attention, two, I started driving before I called him so I could get here faster hoping he would say yes, three, no, I have no idea what those flames were. Is that about right?"

"Yes, exactly."

Marie and Braun heard a rustle in the trees to their left. Braun pulled Marie close. A man in all black clothing, an automatic gun at his side, stood just far enough outside of the trees for them to see him. He spoke in a low voice.

"We saw the crash. Amazing you two survived. Braun come with me, Marie, continue down this road to the farmhouse. Remember, keep your jacket on."

Braun kissed Marie and disappeared in the forest with the man. Marie continued walking toward the farmhouse. She replayed the three lies in her head, imagined how she would say them. She took death breaths to calm herself. She could see the yellow door in the fading light and stopped. *This is it, tonight I may die, Evangeline, be with me.* She gently knocked on the door. She heard no movement or noise inside. Her spine was tingling, she desperately wanted to run back to Braun.

Then, the heavy metal lock on the door slid open; Marie held her breath. The first thing Marie sees is Ivan at the table, his hands tied behind his back. The door shut behind her and Viktor spoke in her ear.

"Brave one, aren't you?"

"Viktor. I told you I would come."

"I didn't hear your car; did you fly here?"

Every nerve ending in Marie's body is stinging with fear, but she swallowed hard and spoke her first lie.

"No, I parked down the road. I didn't want to attract attention."

"*Hmm*, I heard a crash and saw flames over the ridge. Did you see anything?"

"No, but I heard it too. I almost turned back."

"Why is that?"

"I wasn't sure if you had called the HHPS to come after me, maybe, they crashed on the way. Did you call them Viktor?"

Marie surprised herself. Turing power back to herself was a little easier than she thought. Her senses were sharp, her confidence rising. Seeing Ivan tied to the chair made her angry, she used that anger to her advantage. If Viktor wanted a fight, she'd give him one.

"No, I don't have to call them. They will be here, I guess you figured that out."

"OK, then let's talk. Untie Ivan, please."

"You don't give orders here."

"Viktor, you promised Ivan would not be hurt. You're the one with gun. What advantage could he and I possibly have over you? I want us to talk as friends, like we did the last time I was here."

"I'll make tea, and you untie him. We can at least be civilized."

Marie did not wait for a reply, instead she went to the sink, filled the kettle, and turned on the stove.

To her amazement, Viktor untied Ivan who seemed to know this was a ruse. He did not attempt to go after Viktor. He rubbed his wrists and stayed seated and did not speak.

"So, like her you are, Marie. Evangeline could always make kittens out of us. But be careful, I still don't trust you. Not yet."

"I know Viktor. I'm not worried. I know you only want to do what's right and so do I. I know Ivan feels the same."

Ivan nodded in agreement.

Marie filled three cups with tea and for a moment, it felt normal, but the flip flopping of her stomach reminded her, she was there for a very different reason. *Now what, they should have heard our conversation. When are they going to break down the bloody door!* Marie wondered if she needed to be clearer, use words to convey without a doubt Viktor had taken the bait.

"Thank you, Viktor, for untying Ivan. And for allowing us to sit here and talk."

Viktor did not speak. Marie watched as Ivan's eyes turned to the gun which now sat on the table between Viktor and him. He looked at Marie for a sign.

"You seem nervous Marie, why?"

"Of course, I'm nervous. You have a gun, and you've called the HHPS. All I can think of is poor Sarah and how I do not want to wind up like that."

It was risky bringing up Sarah, but Marie was scared, she thought a little authenticity would help the situation. Besides, it would be interesting to know for the record if Viktor was in on that. If he was, she could never forgive him, and that would make letting die Wächter kill him so much easier. That is if she could get the gun away from him.

"I had nothing to do with that. I never meant for Sarah or Hans to be harmed. That was done without my knowledge. You understand?"

"I'm glad to hear it.

"Now, tell me something I want to hear. What is your plan for the letters? How can I help you?"

Marie's heart was pounding, *where the hell are they!* She had not expected things to get this far. They did not talk about what she should say regarding the letters. *They were supposed to be here by now!*

Marie sipped her tea and took her time. She was about to speak when she saw a flash of light outside the window behind Viktor. In that split second, her mind wondered, was it the HHPS or Braun and Die Wächter? She purposefully kept her gaze on her teacup or straight into Viktor's eyes. She could not let him notice she was distracted by something outside.

"I was hoping you had…"

Marie did not get to finish her sentence. Members of die Wächter and Braun burst through the kitchen door. Ivan was able to grab Viktor's gun and quickly backed away from the table as two of the armed men swiftly pulled Viktor's hands behind his back and pushed his head down on the table. Handcuffed, Viktor was thrashing trying to get free and yelling at Ivan in Hungarian until he turned his eyes on Marie.

"I wanted to trust you, you traitor!"

"And I wanted to trust you Viktor, but you lost sight of the truth and your sense of goodness. Beethoven would not have wanted his name dragged through the mud, again, and lies about his Immortal Beloved spread all over the news. You had to have known that. Was it greed, or revenge that made you do this?"

"What do you know of the truth? You are a pawn, Marie; may you rot in hell!"

Viktor was removed from the house and shoved into one of the black SUV's. Ivan, Marie, and Braun were alone. Marie put her hand on Ivan's shoulder, she could see the pain in his eyes. His dearest friend had betrayed him. He looked like a ghost, a man lost without a country, without a friend. Marie wondered what Evangeline would have thought about all this.

"Ivan, I'm so sorry you had to go through this."

"It's all right Marie, in truth, I had my suspicious about him, I just did not want to see it. But the time to mourn lost friendships will have to wait. We don't have much time before the HHPS are swarming my farm. I need to tell you one last secret. Braun, Marie, please sit."

"Marie, I dare not ask you what you will do with the letters as it remains your decision alone. But I must tell you this so that you know all the facts. Evangeline would have wanted you to know, I'm sure of it. She spoke many times of it."

Marie reached for Ivan's hand across the table.

"Tell me, please."

"It was long ago. You had just celebrated your fifth birthday. Evangeline and I were married, not in the legal sense, but we were handfasted in a small chapel near Teplice. My mother's family was Scottish, and she taught me the Celtic traditions she held dear when I was a child. She told me the handfasting ceremony she shared with my father meant more to her than her traditional wedding which she and my father did to please his parents. Evangeline also believed in the rite of handfasting. We knew it was the only way we could be sealed together in God's eyes and in ours. It was our greatest wish."

"I'm not surprised Ivan, it makes me happy."

"What I have to say next is not so easily fathomed. There is a secret, Braun, which perhaps even you do not know about Beethoven's Immortal Beloved. It has been passed down through generations to the oldest female in the line. Evangeline had it, and she trusted me to tell you, Marie. When I invited you to visit me again, it was because I needed to share it with you. I don't believe we have the luxury of time with so many forces plotting against us. I need to tell you here and now."

Braun stiffened his lips and Marie could see the muscles in his face and neck tighten. Whatever Ivan had to say, it is something Braun does not already know, Marie felt sure of that.

"The Immortal Beloved is buried below the earth in a tomb in Teplice, on the grounds of St. John the Baptist Church. Evangeline and I chose the church for our handfasting rite which was performed by a priest I knew since childhood. Of course, we chose this church because we needed to visit the tomb. The instructions given to Evangeline were very specific. We found the entrance to the underground tomb and her coffin. We slid the cement lid off to the side of the coffin. Inside, lie her mummified remains. Just above her right shoulder is a hidden panel. Inside the panel sits a wooden box. The box contains two letters from Beethoven. It is here Evangeline wishes for you to hide the rest of the letters for eternity."

Marie was pacing back and forth in the small kitchen. Braun watched her, but did not speak.

"What is her name?"

"The tomb is unmarked. I truly do not know who she was, Evangeline did not know either. Her identity remains a mystery."

"You're sure no one knows about the tomb? Did Viktor know, did you or my aunt tell him?"

"Never. Marie, you are the first person I have told, and I know for sure Evangeline told no one else, but me. The four of us and of course, the priest are the only ones who know the secret. In all the world, we are the only people who know where the true Immortal Beloved rests. I am telling you the truth."

"Teplice. It seems like historians would have figured this out by now considering how often Beethoven went there."

"Perhaps, but the instructions Evangeline had contained no other information other than how to find the tomb. The town of Teplice would have been a three-day carriage ride or longer from Vienna. It is intentional. Teplice may have been special to him, historians just never put the clues together. They always look at the obvious. Maybe, it was the home of the Immortal Beloved. She may have had family ties there. We will never know."

Chapter Twenty
Vienna, 1826

Beethoven's carriage was well known in Vienna. He could not use it to make this journey. He hired a coach, comfortable, but not so lavish as to call attention to itself. He and Therese Marie sat side by side, their hands intwined for the long journey to Teplice. Two or three days away from a piano, Beethoven would never have permitted it, but for her, there was no sacrifice too great. It was as if time stood still. They talked in the carriage and laughed, Beethoven managing to kiss her as they bumped along rolling hillsides. Stopping at dusk for fresh horses, they spent the night in small Inns where no one recognized him. They dined in their room, and danced, she leading him to the music below muffled by the wood floorboards and they made love. A dream, stolen moments which made up the strong bonds of their love. Beethoven was happy, a feeling the great composer rarely knew. How easily she could tame the constant rage inside him. Never annoyed by his deafness which was profound, she would hold his face in her soft hands and speak so that, he could watch her lips, feel her gentle touch. He would be forever changed in her hands even if only for a fleeting few days.

The church of St. John the Baptist stood stark-white against the dark gray, moody sky at mid-day. This is the place Beethoven wanted her to be buried. Away from the scandals that followed him in Vienna, away from the sour gentleman and gentlewomen who shunned him as he fell out of favor at court. Here, where their love was untainted and pure, would be her final resting place. He wanted to arrange it so he could leave this earth knowing, she would be protected, even in death.

"You've arranged it, I trust."

The young priest was not intimidated by Beethoven, he felt his pain, he saw his anguish and illness. His heart knew the comfort God's grace provided and he was determined to help them.

"Yes, Herr Beethoven, it is all arranged. Would you like to see it?"

Behind the alter is a floor to ceiling, gilded gold and dark wood panel. A single painted wooden crucifix, the image of Christ resigned and sad, hung in the center. The wood panel opened to a dome shaped room. Their footsteps echoed up to the ceiling, like the beat of wings on small birds. The priest motioned for them to move through the dome to the left back wall. A marble façade. On the floor was a metal candelabra, the candles were not lit.

"Please step back."

The candelabra was embedded in the slate floor. With his shoe, the priest pushed a metal lever which barely stood up out of the slate the floor, upward until it clicked. He strained to move the candelabra to the left. When he did, the last column of marble tiles opened downward, revealing a staircase.

"Please take care, the steps are steep."

Beethoven held her hand as they descended the stairs, the light from the torches on the wall making their path easier to navigate. She let out a gasp, Beethoven held her close. The marble tomb looked so like her. The serene figure of a woman supine, hands crossed over the stomach, delicately carved wildflowers lay just under them.

My love, it's so beautiful. But I want to rest forever next to you, though I know it cannot be."

Beethoven did not speak, but exchanged glances with the priest.

"My body will be in Vienna, my heart and soul will always be with you, my love."

The priest gestured to the tomb.

"Inside, there is a panel which holds a box. As instructed, your letters and anything else you wish can be placed here. My dear, you, but need to ask, and I will see it made so."

She turned her face and buried it in Beethoven's chest. She had seen enough. The gesture, the care, the gift of his eternal love was overwhelming. She did not want to think of death, just as a new life was beginning inside her. She would keep the baby a secret, for just a little longer to be sure.

Walking out of the church, they paused at the tin baptismal font at the altar. The inscription held special meaning: *peccata ordinaria in eo abluuntar,* (ordinary sins are washed away in it). Beethoven agreed, certainly forbidden love is the most ordinary sin of the ages. His faith in God was always complicated. At times he despised him for testing him and in the end, taking so much from him. Whatever his feelings about God, a God who has forsaken him, he wanted her to receive the most of his blessings.

Chapter Twenty-One

"We need to get the letters to Teplice. Ivan, do you know anyone there who can help us?"

"Yes, a priest. He is the great, great grandson of the priest who helped Beethoven. He, his father and grandfather before are keepers of the secret, too and have always helped us."

"We should leave now."

"Yes, I agree. Braun and Marie, I pray you make it to the tomb safely."

"Wait, we don't have a car."

Just then, one of the members of die Wächter came into the kitchen.

"You still have the microphone on, forgive us, but we overheard you talking. We have a car you can take. We'll follow you, but keep hidden. If there is any trouble, you won't be alone. Good luck."

He tossed the keys to Braun and left.

Marie wrapped her arms around Ivan, and they held each other for a long moment.

"I'll do my best Ivan and when I return, we will toast Evangeline and start our new lives."

"My dear Marie, I will be here, God willing. Take good care of her Braun, I'm counting on you."

"You know I will. Thank you, Ivan, you are a true friend."

Braun started up the borrowed Jeep and they drove the long dirt driveway away from the farmhouse.

"Braun wait, I just realized, we don't have all the letters. The ones in my bag are at your house and the one Hanna has, do you, have it?"

"Yes, I have it and your letters too."

"But how did you know?"

"Something in my gut told me to put them all together and to keep them close. Maybe, it was the piano, perhaps he likes me after all."

Braun smiled and Marie smiled back.

"Will you keep the ring or put it in the tomb?"

"I'm going to keep it. She wanted me to have it. At least that's what I heard her say to Beethoven. The fact that Beethoven had a tomb made for her with a secret panel, tells me what we are doing is exactly what he wanted. Braun, I cannot imagine my life without you now. I hope you don't mind me saying it."

Braun reached for her hand, took it to his lips and kissed it.

"I've prayed I would hear you say those words. They are true for me too."

Marie settled in for the six-hour drive to Teplice. With Braun at her side, she felt safe. The HHPS would most likely be tracking them, but so was die Wächter. She drifted off to sleep with the tenuous hope die Wächter would protect them. Her dreams were a kaleidoscope of the past, present, and the future. She saw herself as a young girl playing the piano at Evangeline's house, next she was making love to Braun again under the Wild Pear tree just as she did only days ago, and in a shadowy room, she held a child in her arms, a fair-haired boy, tears streaming down her face.

Marie was jolted awake by the screeching of tires, the car spinning. She could see Braun struggling to right the car again.

"What's happening?"

"A truck came at me head on, hold on!"

Braun managed to maneuver the car off the road safely onto the shoulder. Braun's phone chirped with a text message from die Wächter. He quickly tapped a short message back to say they were OK.

"They want to flank us, one car in front and one behind us. I won't argue with that."

"How far away are we?"

"We still have about two hours to go. Anything could happen, I'm glad they are so diligent about following us."

"I just want this to be over. Thank you, my love, for keeping us safe."

Marie reached over and pulled Braun close. They had escaped death together more times than she cared to count. This man, this new life was so different from her past, but Marie needed him, and the rest would just have to play itself out. She longed for the days ahead when she and Braun could live a peaceful life together. *A peaceful life,* she hoped it was possible.

"I'm going to push on now. We *will* get there in time Meine Liebe, trust me."

Braun waited as the head car of die Wächter pulled in front of them. He followed careful to stay close to the speed limit and to keep a distance between the car ahead and the car behind them. His eyes darted to the rearview mirror every few minutes, his senses on high alert now. Marie could see the concentration and the strain in his face. She settled herself in her seat, maybe, if she kept calm, it would help Braun. In her heart she knew neither of them would find calm or restful sleep until the letters were safely sealed in the Immortal Beloved's tomb.

The last two hours of the drive passed without incidence It could have been a random occurrence, some truck driver short on sleep veered into the oncoming lane. It happens. But Braun didn't believe that. He would not leave himself open to surprise again. His hands stayed gripped to the steering wheel as Marie dozed off. His phone chirped and the message came up on the dash screen. "Up ahead exit five."

Braun took exit five and followed the lead car down a dusty dirt road. His GPS navigation showed a different route to the church. It appeared they were skirting the property, entering from the south end. Braun made sure to check the GPS frequently, just in case, he wanted to be ready to take off if he needed to. The lead car turned off its lights and parked. Braun followed suit just as Marie woke up.

"My God, we're here. It's so dark."

"Stay in the car, let's wait for their signal."

The men in the lead car got out and gathered gear from the rear of the SUV. They turned on torch flashlights and

Braun and Marie could see the men in full SWAT gear. One of them approached the car. A knock on the window.

"We're ready to move. You can get out now, we'll give you instructions."

Braun looked at Marie and they both exited the car.

One of the men laid out a map on the hood of Braun's car and shone the exceptionally bright torch light on it.

"We are here. We will flank the church which is here. You two will walk the main road to church. When you get to the door, knock twice, that's it, just twice. Understand?"

'Yes."

"The priest, Alfonso Letti, will greet you and take you to the tomb. We've been in touch with him, he knows exactly what to do. We will stay outside and keep watch. If there is trouble, we'll know, as long you keep your jacket on."

Marie tapped the button on her jacket, the microphone was still there.

"Let's move."

The man handed Braun a torch flashlight and he and Marie headed down the dirt road to the church, Braun squeezing Marie's hand as they walked. As they stood outside the ornate wood doors to the Church, Marie spoke.

"This is it. Give me just a minute to breathe."

Braun held Marie's hand and waited as she took in three, slow, deep breaths.

"OK, let's go."

Braun knocked twice as instructed and stopped. They waited. The sound of shuffling feet and then the click of the heavy lock on the door.

"Good evening, I'm Father Letti, you must be Marie."

"Yes, Father, and this is Braun."

"Come in, please."

Father Letti carried a candle and led them into the church. He walked to the side vestibule and lit two more candles then handed them to Braun and Marie.

"I was instructed not to turn on the lights tonight. I think I like the church better in candlelight anyway, don't you agree? I have been in this parish for fifteen years. My father, his father before him and my great grandfather were all priests here. We are all friends of die Wächter. I never thought the day would come when I would do anything as important as they had done. It is my great honor to help you both. It is God's work, I believe. After all, love is why we are here, a mission of great love."

As Marie listened to Father Letti, she felt a sadness about this mission. Father Letti is correct, it is a mission of love, but it came so many years too late. She wondered if Beethoven was watching them now if he knew his Immortal Beloved would finally be able to rest in peace. Marie decided he must know, after all he led her here with the help of his confidant, the piano.

Father Letti ushered them to the dome room, the back wall, and the entrance to the stairway that will take them far below the church. *This is the same room Beethoven walked with her all those years ago*, Marie thought. Father Letti shuffled his foot to move the lever in the floor. He handed his candle to Braun and pushed the candelabra to the left. The marble column creaked and opened.

"Follow me, but be careful, the stairs are slippery and steep."

She walked lightly, like a ballet dancer hardly making a sound on the slate floor. She did not want to disturb the holy silence in this place. Marie is not particularly religious, but she is deeply spiritual; the power of the unseen has always been a part of her life, even now, the piano is proof of that. Love, however, love is a new feeling for Marie especially the power of love which transcends time as we know it. Marie having never experienced true passionate love, love which prevails over everything in its way, can only hope her instincts are right with Braun. And, she has to believe Beethoven and the piano are guiding her to do as he wished, an enigmatic feeling with no basis in fact. A shiver runs up her spine, she winces, almost dropping her candle.

The narrow stone staircase is tricky, just as the father Letti warned. The cave like stairwell smelled musty and damp. The stairs and the walls are covered in clay-colored dust, and soot marks stained the walls where fire sconces once hung. As they descended, their feet on stone steps echo with a hollow, thundering sound which makes Marie think of Beethoven's woeful music. Moonlight Sonata when played with passion as Beethoven meant it to be, is full of longing and dread. Most people believe it was meant to be a light, uplifting piece, but if you study the music, the way it was written, it is anything but.

It is getting colder and darker. Father Letti hums a melancholy hymn. Marie's eyes are welling with tears, tears for the forbidden love of Beethoven and his Immortal

Beloved, tears for the betrayal of old friends, and for love yet to fully bloom. This journey has taken on a new meaning, a holy pilgrimage of sorts. The events of the past few weeks have made Marie rethink many things including her relationship to God, or her lack of it. How could she not believe in a creator, a force greater than herself, than all humans? If there is no higher purpose, surely the piano would not have communicated with her and surely her dreams which pierced the veil of time between this world and the world of the dead would not have been so real.

Her dreams revealed the past, the truth of Beethoven which no one else in the world knows. Was it the spirit of Beethoven or was it God, revealing to her the truth of life and death? Beethoven is her ancestor, his blood runs in her veins, she is part of him. When she found the ring in the piano, Marie realized the reality of time as we think we know it, means nothing. Her ancestor was reaching for her through the veil, she is connected to him even all these years later. She was meant to find him and to learn the truth, and she was meant to right the wrongs he endured in his time. Is it God who intervened and allowed this to happen? Is it Jesus himself? Beethoven was a nominal catholic with a complicated relationship with God. He spoke to God, and he cursed him in equal measure. There must be a force greater than humankind which connects us to the past and the future and to each other. Otherwise, nothing matters, life would not have meaning. Marie had no doubt she was experiencing something extraordinary, out worldly, and perhaps even holy in this moment. She would make sure the letters were hidden; she would lay down her life for it.

Finally, a stone archway came into view and Father Letti stopped. He lit the candles in a large candelabra and put his candle in the tall metal candlestick just beside the tomb. Marie stood at the entrance to the room, her body seized, she could not move, not yet. The sarcophagus is intricately carved. Marie recognizes her face from her dreams, her serene and beautiful face lovingly etched in warm, creamy marble, the face of the Immortal Beloved, her body small and delicate. Marie takes in the sight of the tomb as tears spill down her face. She motions for Braun to stay where he is, she needs to process this moment her own way, in her own space. A few more moments pass, Marie walks to the tomb. She touches her face feeling the cold, smooth marble under her fingers. She traces the outline of the flowers which lay so gently under her hands.

"I am here, I have your letters. You can rest at peace now, be with him. I will always keep your secret."

Marie stepped back and looked at Father Letti and Braun who stood on either side of the tomb.

"We need to gently slide the lid off at an angle near the top. This way, you can get to the panel where the box sits and place the letters inside. Marie, we will need your help."

Father Letti, Braun, and Marie flank the tomb and began to slowly push the top. Marie pushes hard, but soon realizes the sarcophagi is much heavier than she imagined, she pushes again with all the force she could muster. The sound of sliding marble on marble, hollow and heavy echoes in the room. Inch by inch the top moved until the right shoulder and arm of the Immortal Beloved could be seen. Marie gasped. All three of them stopped to take in the sight of the unnamed woman known only as, the Immortal Beloved.

"I would like to say a blessing now as it is considered sacrilegious to disturb the body after it has been buried. God will forgive us I know, but I must bless her, you understand?"

"Of course, father."

Marie held Braun's hand as the priest began his blessing which he spoke in Latin.

"In the name of the father, son, and holy spirit, we bless you and offer our prayers. May the angles bless and keep you; may you be at peace with Beethoven at the side of our mother Mary, we pray. Amen."

"Amen." Braun and Marie spoke the amen in unison and for the first time in Marie's life, it felt like a genuine prayer.

"I will leave you now for a few moments. The panel is here, as you can see. I ask you to take the utmost care with her, please do not touch her if you can manage it. Place the letters in the box, then we will seal her tomb together. I must ask you to be as swift as you can, we all know there are forces who want to rob her of her peace. I will be just outside the arch, waiting."

Braun and Marie went to her and saw the outline of the panel.

"Braun, my hands are shaking, I think you should open the panel."

"Of course, Meine Liebe."

Braun's hands are large, but he moves with the deft grace of a pianist gently opening the panel without touching her. He slowly lifts out the wood box and places it on top of the sarcophagus.

"Would you like to open it, or shall I?"

"Please," Marie motioned with her hands.

Braun opens the box.

"Two more letters, Braun, did you know about these?"

"I don't think anyone knows about these. Do we dare read them?"

Marie doesn't answer. She doesn't know what to say. She wants desperately to read them, of course, but should they remain the Immortal Beloved's secret? They are hers after all.

"Meine Liebe, look, they are still sealed, Beethoven's seal. It doesn't feel right to open them just to satisfy our own curiosity."

"I agree, but I wonder why they are sealed. Let me see the front."

Braun turns the letters over and Marie gasps.

"My God, they were mailed after his death, she never opened them."

"That means someone else knew about their relationship in her lifetime, someone he trusted to mail the letters, someone very close to him. The priest or maybe, it was someone in my family?"

"Braun, do you think so? That would explain it. But still, why didn't she open them?"

"Perhaps they reached her after her death and the same trusted friend who sent them for Beethoven, made sure they were buried with her. Questions we may never know the answers to."

"So many questions. I think we should put them back along with the others. I don't think the contents were meant to be shared, it's not for us to know."

Marie handed Braun the other letters and he placed them all in the box. Then, gently with great care, he slid the box into the panel and closed the small door.

"Braun, I have to admit, I want to see her face."

"As do I."

Marie pulled her phone out of her pocket, looked at Braun and put her finger to her lips. She remembered she still had the microphone attached to her jacket. She clicked on the flashlight and pointed it into the coffin. Braun bent down next to her; they held their breath as they gazed upon the face of the Immortal Beloved.

The shuffling of Father Letti's feet could be heard coming closer. Marie snapped off her flashlight and they waited.

Berlin, 1846

Therese Marie Amille lies quietly in her bed, her gray curls gracefully encircle her head on the silk pillow. In her hand, she clutches a silver locket with a single lock of hair tucked inside. Beethoven's hair, she cut it off at his bedside a few days before he left her and the world, forever. She dreams of him now, days long past, singing and playing by his side at his faithful piano. Her life since his death was ordinary, she married twice, had children with her husbands, but twenty years or so later, she still years for only Beethoven. She knows she will meet him soon. She prays God is merciful and grants her final wish to be in his arms for eternity.

"Mother, my sweet mother, I can't let you go."

Johannes, her son, is weeping at her bedside side as he has done for days now. He is young and beautiful, his strong chin, brown eyes, and serious expression are so like Beethoven. Therese Marie longs to tell him the truth, but even now, she fears for what it will do to his reputation. In time, the truth of his father's name will be known to him, but for now it must wait.

"Johannes, my son, my heart, take this locket, keep it always. It contains a lock of your father's hair, your real father whose name I cannot speak."

"Oh mother, I wish we had more time."

"We've had a lifetime my son. Your life is laid out before you, a golden road you must walk with dignity and happiness, for I have loved you with all my being. You are so loved, my dear son."

Johannes weeps as his mother takes her last breaths. He knows what her wishes are, in fact, his solicitor waits with the funeral carriage outside to take her to her final resting place. Johannes wonders why she chose to be buried in Teplice. To his knowledge, she had never visited there and yet, it means the world to her. She took him there a few years ago and showed him the vault made just for her. She never told him who commissioned it. Johannes suspected his real father was a man of some wealth, had some standing in the city, but he could not find any clues as to who he was. He wished his mother would tell him, even now as she prepared to leave this earth, she kept the secret, a sacred secret she called it. Johannes loved his mother and trusted her. He knew she was protecting him and yet, he was a young man who needed to know his father, even if only his name. Therese Marie made Johannes promise to fulfill her wishes and he agreed, he would make sure she was not disappointed.

As dusk falls and the shadows retreat into dark corners, Therese Marie takes her last breath and whispers one final word, *Ludwig*, and she is gone.

Chapter Twenty-Two

Braun and Marie are seated on at stone bench next to the sarcophagus holding hands. The candlelight gives a soft glow to the room and Marie is grateful to have time to be with her, the Immortal Beloved, for the last time. *Does she know what has happened, how close they came to losing the letters and the secret of her legacy?* Marie's heart tells her she knows, and maybe, she had something to do with the outcome. The Immortal Beloved, her power transcends time, Marie is sure of that much.

"I think we should close the sarcophagus now, yes?"

"Yes, father, of course."

Braun, Marie, and Father Letti, push the lid back into place. Marie stands next to the sarcophagus, her hand tracing the folds of her gown for a long moment.

"It's hard to leave her."

"Yes, I know, I feel the same. When this is finally over, we will visit her again, together."

Marie agreed, but both she and Braun knew it was too risky to return here.

"I'd like that."

As they leave the soft darkness of the tomb, Marie shields her eyes from the sun, bathing the church in bright yellow light as a new day begins in Teplice. *What happens next?* Marie's heart is pounding. Will she and Braun truly be able to move forward together? She takes Braun's hand and leans into him.

***

Hanna waits anxiously at the door to the Hungarian National Museum, her home, and her life's sole purpose. She sees Braun and Marie take the steep steps to the door and holds her breath.

"I'm so glad you are both safe."

Hanna hesitates to embrace Braun, but Marie goes to her, arms outstretched.

"Thank you, Hanna, let's go to your place and talk."

Settled in Hanna's comfortable living room, Marie remembers the last time they were there. Her heart was so full of doubt and anger then. Now, she is grateful for Hana's friendship, and she feels a kinship with her knowing what she sacrificed to do the right thing on both accounts, letting Braun go and giving her the letter she held so dear.

"I can't believe Viktor would betray us this way, I'm happy he is in custody. Still, it's hard to lose old friends. So much has changed in such a short amount of time. I wonder what our lives will be like now that Beethoven's secret is safe forever."

"We can pray it will be safe forever. At least we know in our lifetimes, we did our best to preserve his legacy. That's all we can do."

"Ah, Braun, so practical as always. I think you need Marie; she brings color to your world. We both know you need it."

Marie and Hanna shared a laugh, Braun smiled.

"What will you do now, Marie? I assume you will stay in Budapest, yes?"

"I'd like to, yes. I have to navigate the emigration process, but for now my Visa is still good for a few months."

Braun looked at Marie, his eyes said what his heart yearned for; he wanted to marry her, emigration would not be an issue. Marie knew he would not bring it up in front of Hanna, but it was plain to see Hanna knew what was on their minds.

"Ah well, I predict there will be another way for you to stay here permanently. Let's toast to the future."

Hanna held up her glass and the three of them toasted to the future, a future Marie felt excited about for the first time in her life.

"I'd like to go to the piano for a moment, if you don't mind."

"Of course, Meine Liebe, I thought you might. Hanna and I need to review the preparations for the new exhibit next month. Take your time."

"Good idea, Braun. We will walk out with you on our way to the office."

Marie entered the piano room as she had dozens of times in the last few weeks. The piano sat silent, waiting. She expected to feel its longing and maybe, even gratitude, embrace her. She wasn't sure how to approach it which felt strange to her. After all, they had become so close, like best friends, like soldiers in battle they shared an uncommon bond. But today, the piano looked ordinary, it felt inert. Marie's heart was in her throat. *Could he be gone, without a goodbye? Does he know how much I care for him?*

She sat on the bench gently laying her hands on the keys, closing her eyes silently calling to him. She felt a warmth under her fingers, the room no longer felt sterile and cold.

"Ah you are here, my friend, I missed you. She is safe, the letters are with her. Beethoven's legacy and wishes are fulfilled. You don't need to worry anymore; you can rest now."

As Marie began to play, the piano responded by emitting warm, whole tones, hope and light were in every note. Marie's eyes welled with tears.

Thank you, heart of my heart.

Marie heard the words and stopped playing, her emotions getting the best of her.

"I don't want to leave you. I will be living here in Budapest; you may have figured that. Can I come see you from time to time?"

My sweet Marie, I have played every note, sung every woeful feeling inside my soul. I wish to be silent, to leave the realm between the living and the dead, to be with him and her, if such a thing is possible. Like his music, this song of our love will never end, but I will no longer be here. This wood and wire instrument will be here for you, but I must go. Marie, never forget you are our love through the ages, transcending time. Think of me, long for me. Your faithful friend will hear you. It's time for you to love the living as you have loved me. Go to him, make him yours, live in the present. We will meet again in another world. Love sweet Marie, love is all. Goodbye, heart of my heart.

Marie wept sitting on the piano bench for what seemed like hours. She knew he was right, his soul needs rest. She had to move forward with the living, her new life laid before her like a colorful mosaic carpet replacing the quiet gray life she used to lead. Time did not stop; it merely revealed its infinite reach to her. She would be forever changed.

Slowly walking the long corridor to elevator, Marie heard the piano. Moonlight Sonata, but it was not played with longing and pain; it felt hopeful and light, as it echoed throughout the museum.

"Goodbye, my friend."

Chapter Twenty-Three

Braun's house has become a refuge for Marie. Thanks to the butler and house staff, it's always warm and inviting, but more than that, Marie feels safe here. Her heart is full, she admits only to herself she could easily call this house home for the rest of her life. As she sips whiskey, she is drawn to the painting over the mantel again. The resemblance is uncanny. *It can't be the Immortal Beloved, is it Evangeline, who is it?* Marie's mind is churning, the painting seems to hold her gaze as if the woman does not want her to look away. Marie pushes a small club chair in front of the fire and settles in; the perfect spot for studying the painting. In a style akin to John Singer Sargent, the intimate mood of the painting captivates; the longer you study it the more it reveals. Subtle and rich jewel tones blend, the delicate texture of the brush strokes, and the light which seems to change and move as the day progresses to night commands your attention. The portrait is lifelike, the woman appears to live and breathe as the soft blush on her arms and face seem to glow from within her body. But the expression on her face is not serene. As if she was caught in a moment of reflection and urgency, her eyes wide, her mouth slightly open, she is revealing a fleeting moment which is part of her larger story. There is depth and emotion in her face and the way her body is turned directly facing the artist. She is not demure beguiling her lovely face and lithe body, she is formidable in her directness. Lost in her thoughts, Marie is uneasy. The woman in the painting is an important piece of Beethoven's history, she is sure of it. The question she does not want to ask herself is, why has Braun not mentioned it? The portrait is right here, in his living room, he sees it every day. If it is Evangeline, who commissioned it, and why would Braun have it?

The events of the past few weeks have made Marie wary. There could be a very ordinary explanation for the painting, not everything has to be a layered mystery. She reminds herself her senses are heightened, that's all. She's been in flight or fight mode for so long now, she is skeptical of everything. Except for Braun's love for her, she feels it in her bones, this man truly loves her.

"Meine Liebe, are you cold, I'm sorry, I will turn up the heat."

"No, Braun, thank you, I just like sitting in front of the fire, I hope you don't mind I moved the chair."

"Not at all, tear down walls if you like, this your house too, I want you to feel this is your home, our home."

"Braun, tell me about this portrait."

Marie gestured to the painting above the mantel with her whiskey glass, asking the question as nonchalant as she could manage.

Braun pushes the matching club chair next to Marie and sat down holding his whiskey tumbler in both hands. His gaze was toward the floor, not the painting. He did not speak right away. Marie has learned to wait, to give him time, but it usually means he has something else to tell her, something else about her life she never knew. Marie sits cross-legged in the chair, mustering her patience.

"You recognize the face, yes?"

"Yes, is it Evangeline?"

"I can't say. As I told you, my father told me our great grandfather commissioned it and it was never to leave this house. A friend of the family who agreed to sit for the portrait in hopes it could be sold to raise funds for the museum. He never mentioned the woman's name. When my father died, the portrait was found locked in a hidden library in his private rooms in the museum. My brothers and I had our hands full trying to take care of the museum, the accounts, and the donors after he died. I do not see a signature of the artist or date. It's a mystery."

"So it can't be Evangeline. Then who is she?"

"I wish I knew."

Marie and Braun sat in silence for a while as the logs in the fireplace crackled. Marie still had so many questions. The expression on the woman's face troubles Marie, it looks strained and frightened.

"Braun, I lived with Evangeline most of my life, I knew her face very well. The way she is painted, the expression on her face, it's… strained and almost pleading. Maybe, it's because this woman looks so much like her but, I sense she was not happy about sitting for this portrait."

Braun stands and stares at the painting. He walks to the right and then to the left, he leans in to look closer.

"I see now, perhaps you are right. There is an urgency of some kind in her expression. I wonder why? I have an idea. Stay here, I will be right back."

Braun is carrying a large ladder over his shoulder. He sets it down in front of the fireplace and calls for the butler to help.

"I can lift it off the hooks and slide it down to you two, one on each side. When you have it on the floor, we will lay it against the couch. I want to see the back."

Braun climbs the ladder and deftly lifts the heavy portrait up and off the large hooks. As he slides it down to Marie and the butler, they catch it and place it upright on the floor. Braun leans it against the couch the back facing them, careful to make sure only the frame is touching the couch and not the painting itself. At first glance the back is unremarkable, the wood stretcher bars securely nailed in the heavy gilt frame, paint splatters on the edges of the wood stretcher bars and the canvas which is a cream color now from age.

"Braun look!"

Marie points to the corner where there appears to be a pocket made of canvas glued to the bottom right of the frame. Braun carefully inspects it and reaches in with one finger.

"There's something inside."

Braun lifts out a small silk bag which looks like it has been sewn shut. The butler reaches into his pants pocket and pulls out a small pocketknife. Braun slits open the bag and the diamond and ruby brooch, the same one the woman is wearing in the painting falls on the carpet. No one moves for a beat or two. Braun kneels and retrieves the brooch. The butler gathers the ladder and leaves Marie and Braun alone.

"It's exquisite, is it real?"

"I'm sure it is, knowing my family. But why keep it hidden?"

Marie gently takes the brooch from Braun and holds it under the lamp light, turning it on all sides.

"Braun, I'm no expert, but this looks very old, older than my aunt at the time this must have been painted. Was it in your family, handed down perhaps to your father?"

"I do not know. I've never seen it before. But you are right it is not a modern piece. I know someone who can help authentic and date it, an old family friend from one of the most respected authentication houses in the country. She also very discreet, I will call her in the morning.

Chapter Twenty-Four
Vienna, 1835

Therese Marie is anxious, scratching mercilessly at her arms and neck. Her skin crawls when she is nervous and being married to Count Marchant has given her many reasons to be nervous. Her arms are raw, and blotches have formed on her delicate porcelain skin. The lavender oil cream she uses in excess tames the burning and itching, but it is all gone. She will have to implore one of her maids to run to the village to purchase more.

Therese Marie's tiny frame is burdened by the heavy weight on her hips. She begrudges the child she carries, her second with the Count.

"Enduring childbirth is a curse of the male, female marriage right," her dear friend, the enigmatic Anne Lister, likes to say and Therese Marie agrees. If she could not produce heirs to continue the Count's family line, she would not be here. She remembers this fact as bile creeps into her throat. Therese Marie is fond of her children, but clearly Johannes is her favorite, perhaps the only child she truly loves as he is the child of Beethoven, her one and only true love.

Her marriages were a farce, manufactured by her father to keep her from becoming an outcast of society, an unwed woman shunned and living in the streets. He arranged for her to marry her first husband in record time after learning she was pregnant. She never revealed the name of the father of her bastard child, even under the cruelest of duress from her family. Besides, it did not matter, the only thing that mattered to her father was that she be properly wed to avoid a costly scandal. Poor Count Marchant, her father persuaded him to marry Therese Marie with same urgency after her first husband died. He didn't trust her to live the life of a restrained widow.

Now, ten years later, Therese Marie is bearing her second child with the Count. She was pregnant with his first soon after they married and gave birth to a lovely little girl with blonde curls. But she grew to be a witless, spoiled brat whom her father dotes on as if she was soon to be queen. Therese Marie has no influence on her and relents to the governess to care for her. Meanwhile, she dreams of leaving them all in the middle of the night, just she and Johannes. But how would they live?

"Come my dear, where is the dress I gave you for the portrait? I want Sir Illes to see you in it."

Count Marchant is a vapid man with no more personality than a bronze statue. Can't he see she is heavy with child? Even so, Therese Marie is obliged to do as he asks. The black velvet dress is heavy and to her distaste, too large for her even in her condition. Her maid, Carenza, helps her get dressed, smoothing the velvet here and there, with envious hands. Therese Marie knows Carenza is young, but she wanted to help her family. Carenza's mother was a good friend to Therese Marie when she first moved to Vienna with the Count. In fact, Volta was the only woman who made her feel welcome. They became good friends.

Therese Marie gestures for Carenza to bring her jewel box to her. She takes out the brooch, encrusted with diamonds and rubies, shaped like a piano. Carenza gasps. Beethoven gave her this brooch so soon after they met. It was scandalous for her to accept it and even more scandalous to begin an affair. Beethoven, one of the worlds most enlightened and talented musicians was also a madman. That's what the newspapers wrote of him. Throughout his life, a constant volley of articles kept him in the public eye; articles praising his genius one day and articles castigating his madness the next. He wasn't mad, he was deaf, a condition the people who shunned him had no inkling about.

"Madame, what a jewel, I have never seen you wear this. Did the Count just present it to you recently?"

"No, he did not. This was a gift, from a friend a long time ago."

"I wish I had such friends."

"Please, speak no more of it. Help me get downstairs, Carenza."

"Ah, my dear there you are. Please allow me to introduce, Ferenc Jozef Illes, the esteemed director of the Hungarian National Museum."

"Madame, my pleasure."

"Good evening, Mr. Illes. Please excuse me, this dress is very heavy, and, in my condition, I must sit."

"What do you think Mr. Illes? Won't my stunning wife make the most exquisite model for Monsieur Ingres?

I am forever in your debt arranging for him to paint her portrait. I intend to make a substantial donation to the museum, one which I hope will afford my name on one of your exhibit rooms."

"Of course, Count. With your generous gift, the museum will expand and will at once employ the services of an expert piano technician to bring Beethoven's 1817 Broadwood into fine playing form again, the prize piece in our museum. We shall hold a great ball in your honor to celebrate."

Therese Marie's heart pounded erratically as the child within her kicked her sides, and she collapsed into the settee. The mere mention of his name in the same breath as her pedestrian husband, made her ill. The Count rushed to get her maid as Ferenc went to her side.

"Madame, I am sorry if this is all too much for you."

"Thank you, sir, I will be fine. A woman in my condition should be in bed, but my husband has these fanciful ideas."

Ferenc Illes, knew about Therese Marie and Beethoven, of course. After all, he paid for the composer to live the life of a gentlemen. He knew their love was to remain a secret and although he was tempted many times, he never revealed what he knew. If given half a chance, he would seduce Therese Marie himself, she was indeed an exquisite woman, even in her advanced stage of pregnancy, Ferenc was aroused by her.

Therese Marie was uncomfortable as Ferenc held her hand for far too long than was customary. She yanked her hand away. Therese Marie had no idea he knew about her and Beethoven, if she did, her life may have been different. But Beethoven kept many secrets, the secret of his largest benefactor, one of them.

Ferenc knew the painting would be worth a fortune, no matter who the subject was. Jean Augste Dominique Ingres was one of the most sought after, popular oil painters of the time. Ferenc had enough clout and money, to convince him to paint Therese Marie's portrait. In return, the Count would fund a project near to Ferenc's heart and the heart of Budapest. Therese Marie was indeed a strikingly pretty woman, that was a bonus. But Ferenc was captivated by her brooch. He stared at it, coveting it.

"May I compliment your stunning brooch, madame. I have not seen something so rare in quite a while. The Count has good taste."

Ferenc, an expert in antique jewelry knew very well the Count had not purchased the brooch. Even with his wealth, it is beyond the Count's pocket to afford such a priceless antique.

"This was not a gift from my husband. It has been in my family for many years, sir."

Therese Marie looked at Ferenc and her eyes burning into his. Without speaking she beseeched him to not mention the brooch and to not press her further. Ferenc knew in that instant it was a gift from Beethoven. He decided he would own it, no matter the cost. Therese Marie knew no matter how much she abhorred her husband, she had to sit for the portrait so the beloved piano, the piano which knew her touch and Beethoven's, the piano which held their secrets, would be brought out into the open. She must see it again!

***

Braun and Marie retired early. As Braun undressed Marie, kissing her neck, her shoulders, and her breasts, she pulled him close whispering how much she wanted him, she could not wait. They made love for hours as the moon rose high in the sky. As the curtains fluttered in the soft summer breeze, Braun got up, went to the dresser, and took the brooch out of the silk bag. He placed it on Marie's chest and the rubies glowed like liquid fire in the candlelight.

"It's the most beautiful thing I have ever seen."

"As are you, it's yours now."

"Braun, I cannot accept it. It's a family heirloom, it's yours."

"And what would I do with it if I cannot give it to the woman I love. It's yours Marie, as am I."

After breakfast, Ms. Colette Izchec arrived to inspect the brooch.

"Colette, how nice to see you again, please come in. This is Marie."

Colette Izchec looks chic in her black crepe suit, her shiny gray hair in a blunt-cut bob. She has known Braun's family for many years and her business is one of the most respected art and antique houses in the country. She walks with a grace and confidence of someone who has been wealthy and independent all her life.

"Ms. Izchec we are so grateful you could be here today. I have heard such good things about your work."

"Ah, Marie, please call me Colette. I am so pleased to meet you; you look familiar somehow."

Braun and Marie exchange glances. Marie stands next to the painting of Evangeline.

"It could be you are thinking of my Aunt Evangeline, the woman in this painting."

Colette does not speak, but looks at Braun and Marie, carefully formulating her words before she says them.

"My dears, I do not think that is Evangeline Vuillard."

"You knew her?" Marie cannot help, but blurt out.

"I did, perhaps that is why you look so familiar to me. The woman in the painting resembles both of you, but it is not her, I am sorry."

So many questions ran through her head. Marie sits, breathing a heavy sigh. Another rabbit hole, another dead end.

"Marie, Evangeline spoke of you often. I think she would be so pleased to know you are here in Budapest at last, her home, the place she loved most in the world. She and I saw this painting only once and for only for precious few seconds. Braun, your father was doing renovations. Josef invited me here to look at something a generous donor gifted the museum. Evangeline was with me, and we saw the painting being wrapped and carried away to storage. Later, I remarked at the uncanny resemblance Evangeline and the woman shared. The remark seemed to rattle her. We were to spend the day shopping in Budapest, I dragged her with me to see your father promising it would take no more than fifteen minutes. She was visibly uncomfortable here, but I did not press her. She was completely herself the rest of the day. I'm afraid that's all I know about it. If she had been the model for this, I would have known."

Marie is visibly frustrated. Braun decides it's best to start at the beginning, with the brooch.

"Colette, here is the brooch we want to show you. As you can see, the woman in the painting is wearing it."

Colette removes a magnifying loop from her bag, a portable, high-tech, foldable light and sets it up on the side table next to her chair. She lays down a piece of black velvet and places the brooch on it. She carefully inspects the extravagant piece, turning it over and over taking her time. Using a thin silver stick, similar in size to a large toothpick, she taps at many of the gems, especially, the rubies. She stops and ponders what she has seen. Next, she turns the brooch on its back and looks at it through her loop, slowly, inspecting every centimeter.

"This is quite old, eighteenth century, Georgian, I am sure of it. It was obviously custom made, commissioned by someone with great wealth and taste, it's quite extraordinary. It bears a jeweler's mark I know well, one of the top designers in Europe from the seventeen hundreds to the early twentieth century. The same house commissioned by royalty to make hallmark gems, some which reside in the Tower of London and the Louve. It's a pity the family did not continue to carry on the name. It is also engraved, here, along the bottom curve which is wider in the back to accommodate the marking. It says, *Beloved.*

I don't know how you came to possess this piece, but it belongs in your museum, it is quite rare."

Braun and Marie do not respond.

"I will also tell you the painting is of the same era."

"Colette, I would never question your expertise, but it is a surprise to us. My father never told me about the painting or the brooch. In fact, it was hidden behind the painting all these years."

"Well, I suspect you have some research to do then. For now, you should have both pieces properly appraised and insured to the teeth. Braun, the value of the brooch is upward of a few million forints at least, I would imagine. The painting is an original Jean Auguste Dominique Ingres am sure of it. It will need to be authenticated as well, of course. But mark my words, it is also worth a small fortune. It further confirms the woman is not Evangeline as it would have been painted in the 1800s."

"But there is no artist's signature, it is unsigned and therefore hard to authenticate, yes?"

"But this painting is signed. Look, here."

Colette moved very close to the portrait and pointed to a mark just above the bottom right, almost imperceptible to the human eye. The faint outline of the letter, "I" in a very ornate style painted in dark blue.

"My God, how did you see that?"

"Easy my dear, I have seen it before. Authentication will verify of course, but I do believe you have an original Jean-Auguste Dominique Ingres on your hands. No doubt commissioned directly from him in the eighteenth century.

It's much larger than his usual works, painted later in his life, and as I say, worth a fortune."

Braun and Marie could not respond. Colette could see they were astonished beyond words. She began to pack her things in her sleek black leather bag. She knew they would need time to process what she had just told them. As is the way with truly valuable art, most people are not aware of the significance or the value of what they have. It's a shock of sorts. Colette has witnessed this many times in her career.

"Colette, could this have been painted say between 1827 and 1846?"

"Yes, indeed, Ingres died in Paris in 1867 I believe, so yes, your dates might be correct. But if I may ask, why those dates in particular? Do you know who the woman is?"

"I have a theory, but it's no more than that. I'm just interested obviously because she resembles my aunt so much."

"Yes, I'm sure you are. I would suggest you research your hunch and let the authenticator know what you have uncovered. The provenance of the pieces is critically important, as you might imagine."

"Do you know much about the classical composers, Beethoven for example?"

"It is an area where I lack expertise. However, my brother is well versed in Beethoven and many other composers. Do you think these pieces are connected to Beethoven?"

Braun is visibly uncomfortable with Marie sharing this information. Marie decides to let the question drop.

"I think you are correct Colette; we have our research to do. I cannot thank you enough for coming out here and sharing your expertise with us. We are very grateful."

"Of course, please call me when you would like the formal appraisals arranged. I would not wait, as I say, you are sitting on a goldmine here. Thank you for allowing me the great honor of seeing these truly stunning pieces. I hope you consider exhibiting them in your museum someday."

Colette sped away in her cherry-red Ferrari and Braun and Marie need a drink. Bran pours them each a scotch and they sit in front of the painting.

"It's her, you believe it is too, right?"

"I do Meine Liebe, but it only raises more questions for both of us. For me, questions about my family, how they were connected to this, questions I have no way of finding answers to now."

"Maybe, your brother knows something? Do you think we should show him these pieces?"

"I don't think so. If my older brother were alive, he may have been able to help, not that he would have, but my younger brother knows less than me, I'm afraid."

Chapter Twenty-Five
Budapest, 1976

Ferenc Braun Illes sipped his whiskey and smiled to himself. Today was the day he waited for, the day he would lay the path to the last conquest of his life. All his power and money, his family's standing in his beloved Budapest afforded him much. He allowed himself to indulge in frivolous pleasure now and then and to enjoy the spoils of his lineage. He lived a conservative life; or so it appeared to those on the outside. He adhered to a strict code of patriotic duty and conduct. But now, at seventy-two-years old, he would have his heart's desire.

In precisely one hour, the young master painter, Gerald Kelly, would arrive to collect his advance to paint her, the obsession of his life, Evangeline Vuillard. And afterward, He would have her, any way he pleased. His fingers tingled with anticipation at stroking her delicate face, her peach skin and feeling the roundness of her breasts in the palm of his hand. Yes, he would have her to himself and perhaps, she would want him just a little.

Evangeline stood in the garden at Ivan's farm. Her place of true happiness and solace. Ivan was the love of her life, his gentle voice, his handsome face, and his tender love for her were all she ever dreamed of. At his farm, she could pretend this was her life, tending to the goats and chickens, planting lettuce and carrots, cooking for Ivan and making love in his small bed every night. She forgot about America and the advances of her third Cousin Anthony whom she loathed. He was aggressive and manipulative using their heritage as a pawn in his scheme to get her into bed. Evangeline knew of her linage, of Beethoven's secret, a secret which ran in her veins. How could Anthony imagine she would sleep with him to bear a child, to keep the linage alive? That's what he expected, but Evangeline had other plans. She would emigrate to Hungary and become Ivan's wife and never set foot in America again.

Tonight, she let Ivan talk her into a fundraising event in Budapest at the Hungarian National Museum. She wanted to see Beethoven's 1817 Broadwood pianoforte for herself and this was the perfect opportunity. Luckily, she brought her favorite black dress which would do nicely for the event. She wondered how Ivan would look in his sharp black suit and shivered with anticipation at the fun they would have at the grand party and later, laughing and talking then letting herself become lost in his eyes making love until dawn. These were the most cherished days of her life; Evangeline would stay here forever if only Ivan would ask her to marry him.

The museum was lit up against the black night sky, black limos their lights glistening on the wet cobblestones, the throngs of people dressed to the nines making their way up the stone steps to the museum. Evangeline was happy, Ivan on her arm she felt like a queen.

Inside the museum, a trio of musicians played softly as guests mingled and drank champagne. A soft chime sounded, the lights dimmed, the evening's presentation was about to begin. Ivan and Evangeline found their seats in the ornate theatre. Ferenc Illes was exceptional. His gift of public speaking was evident, the crowd was at his mercy and Evangeline had no doubt donations would be rolling in. Afterward, everyone proceeded to the lobby for cocktails before the live auction. Evangeline was watching the harpist with her deft fingering of the strings making the notes sing from the gilded gold harp.

"My dear, please let me introduce you to Ferenc Illes, the director of the museum."

Evangeline took a step back as the fiercely handsome, stoic man stood before her. His eyes widened and he took just a beat too long to speak.

"Ah, hello, my name is Evangeline, very nice to meet you."

"Evangeline, I'm so pleased you are here. Please, enjoy the party, and I do hope we will meet again soon."

Ferenc turned and politely walked away. Evangeline sensed a sinister coolness in his touch, she pulled her silk shawl tighter around her shoulders.

"He's creepy, I didn't realize you knew him."

"His family is like royalty here in Budapest, they started the museum and they have always controlled it. Remember, I worked in government; I had many meetings with him. He's very powerful."

"Well, if I never see him again, it will be too soon."

"My dear, you look shaken, are you all right?"

"That man, he gives me the oddest feeling, he is dangerous Ivan, be careful."

"I'm sorry he makes you uncomfortable, I know you well enough to know you are probably right. I've done my duty here; would you like to leave?"

"Yes, please, thank you, my love."

The next morning, Evangeline felt peaceful. Waking up on Ivan's farm was heaven. She got dressed and started making breakfast, Ivan was up hours ago and would be starving by now.

"Why did you let me sleep, I could have had breakfast ready before you went out, I'm sorry."

"Watching you sleep in my bed is the single most important thing in my day. Besides, I kept you up too late, no?"

Ivan laughed and playfully pinched Evangeline's hip, a gesture she loved. As they drank coffee in the sunny kitchen, Evangeline let herself daydream, after all she was still so young, only twenty-five years old and life still held promise and innocent possibility. Ivan would ask her to marry him, they would have the ceremony at the little church in town and the reception on the farm. She would never have to see Anthony again.

The blaring ring of the telephone on the kitchen wall broke her daydream. Ivan had just kissed her cheek and was headed back to the goats. Evangeline did not like answering the phone, it wasn't her house, not yet. But the ring had startled her and out of habit, she answered.

"Hello, Ivan Karoly residence."

"Is this the lovely Evangeline?"

Evangeline did not respond.

"This is Ferenc Illes from the museum. I hope I am not disturbing you."

"Mr. Illes, Ivan is out on the farm, shall I tell him to call you back?"

"No, that's quite all right, it's you I would like to speak to. I have some important information regarding your legacy, the legacy of Beethoven. I can have a car pick you up in the morning and we can meet in my office."

Evangeline could not speak. *How does he know?*

"Forgive me, I know I must have surprised you. I mean you no harm, bring Ivan with you if you like."

"I will meet you, tomorrow then."

Evangeline hung up the phone, and to stifle the scream she could not silence, she covered her mouth with her hands. She had not told Ivan about her lineage; she did not want to create trouble for him. She knew in Budapest, Beethoven was one of the most revered figures in their history, to expose the truth would change both of their lives and the last thing Evangeline wanted was to change anything about Ivan's life. She would go to Budapest, hear him out and leave it at that. Ivan did not need to know.

Evangeline made an excuse about seeing an old college friend, an actress shooting a film in Budapest, they would have lunch, shop, and catch up. The limo was sent by her, an extravagance Ivan knew Evangeline would never spring for. Evangeline arrived at the museum and the driver walked her to the door. She was met by another man who said he was to escort her to Mr. Illes' office. As they rode the elevator to the sixth floor, Evangeline could feel her stomach doing flip flops. She was not a very political person, she most likely would not be able to finesse this highly sophisticated man. She could not imagine what he had to say, she hoped it was something wonderful.

"My dear, please come in."

Ferenc's office is palatial filled with paintings and tapestries. He ushered Evangeline to the couch near a crackling fireplace and offered her a glass of whiskey. Evangeline's first instinct was to refuse, but she needed something to settle her nerves, so, she accepted.

"I honestly cannot imagine why I am here, Mr. Illes."

"Please call me Ferenc. Do you know the history of my family?"

"I know very little, just what Ivan told me regarding the museum."

"Yes, it is my life, it has been my family's passion and mission for almost two hundred years. I have done much research on Beethoven as you might imagine. I know about the secret child, the real Immortal Beloved, and I know you are a direct descendant. Does that surprise you?"

"I am surprised, and I cannot imagine what it is you need to tell me."

"My dear, I don't *need* to tell you anything, I choose to. There is a big difference. Would you like me to continue, or should I have my man take back to the farm?"

Evangeline refused to let this man intimidate her. He was obviously attracted to her, maybe, she could use that to her advantage. She finished the rest of the whiskey in her glass and remained silent.

"Good. There is a certain underground group in Budapest that has operated for decades, they seek to expose the truth of the Immortal Beloved for financial gain and to ruin my family. They too, know about you and will sooner or later kidnap you and make you give them the letters you have. I can make all that go away. I can make sure your secret and the letters are never found and that you and Ivan can live in peace on his farm, if that's what you really want. Would you like that?"

Evangeline did not ask, she just poured herself another glass of whiskey and drank it in one gulp.

"Yes, I would like that very much. I assume it will come at a great cost. What will it be?"

"You surprise me, you are much more sophisticated than I gave you credit for. Yes, there is a price, but it's not so steep. Let me explain. It's simple really, as a very rich and powerful man, I am used to getting what I want, and I want you. Specifically, I want two things from you. I have commissioned a portrait of you to be painted, wearing a very fine, vintage black velvet gown from the museum vault. It was her dress you see, and was found among Beethoven's possessions in a trunk after he died. We managed to acquire it and it's far too precious to exhibit, but you my dear would be stunning with it draped around your naked body. Oh, and there's one more thing you will wear, a diamond and ruby brooch which you can keep if you agree to my terms."

"And what is the second thing you want from me, Mr. Illes."

"I want you in my bed for one night, one night only unless you would like to revisit it. In which case, I would be happy to entertain you anytime, my dear Evangeline."

Evangeline would not give in to the knot weaving its way up her throat, she will not let him see her squirm. The whole thing is so absurd, she would not give in to blackmail.

"When you say, it was hers, you mean the Immortal Beloved? But how could you know that for sure?"

"Good question! One I will not answer for you or anyone else. You look exactly like her; did you know that? She was a singular woman, more than beautiful, and I want what he had."

"If I don't agree, I assume you will let this secret society have their way with me or will you lead them to me? If so, I think the authorities might have something to say about it."

Ferenc laughs, loudly and gets to refill the whiskey decanter. He sits next to Evangeline, far too close for comfort and fills her glass.

"Am I so wretched you cannot conceive of making love to me. No, don't answer, just know this. I would make it my life's endeavor to make you happy. If you were mine, you would cry out in ecstasy every night, I would give you everything I have. Can your farmer do that?"

Evangeline does not speak. Ferenc reaches for the button on her blouse and manages to open it with one deft movement.

"Sublime, you are, you should be treated like a queen. Give me a chance."

Evangeline is weighing her options. He is magnetic in a way, but he is also crazy. She knows she cannot play the insulted female in this moment; she must be cleverer than that. She's delt with artists who letch after her at parties she should be able to handle this.

"Perhaps you could give me just a taste, now."

Stunned, Ferenc does not move. Evangeline brings her lips to his face, brushing her breast on his arm and whispers into his ear.

"I am not so easily moved, work harder."

To her surprise, Ferenc kisses her and gently lays her down on the couch, he is strong, but gentle and her mind is spinning with what to do next. He reaches under her skirt, and she feels herself respond, letting him fondle her. Then, he stops, helps her up and straightens his tie.

"You are far too special to be had on a couch in some office, even you know that. Say yes, and we can continue in a much more enjoyable way. But to be direct, yes, if you deny me, I will let the HHPS find you and do as they will. With one phone call I can change your life. You decide if it will be for the better."

"Your terms are clear. Now, let me spell out mine, or did you think this would be one sided?"

Ferenc is amused and Evangeline is getting to him.

"Please."

"No one will ever know of our, arrangement. No one, you must promise on the lives of your sons. The letters will always be mine and when I die, you and your sons will make sure my heir receives them. This you must solemnly promise, or I will not concede, and you will not survive this unscathed. I have more resources at my disposal than you might imagine."

"Of course, the painter will know, but I can take care of that with enough money. I promise Evangeline, you have my word."

Evangeline arrived back at Ivan's farm just after dusk. She sees Ivan hard at work in the shed, his blonde curly hair glistening in light. Her heart is in pieces. She cannot do this to him, the one true love of her life. She had another option, but it will take all the courage she can muster. She must tell Ivan about Beethoven and the letters.

Chapter Twenty-Six

The phone rings and Marie jumps. She is lost in her thoughts trying to untangle the mystery of the woman in the painting and the brooch. All roads lead back to Braun's family, it's uncanny the way things worked out. Of all the people in Budapest, Marie finds love with the one man in all the world who could understand what she was going through, who understands what it means to have a family lineage, a legendary family lineage.

"Marie, I'm afraid I must go to the museum this morning. Would you like to come into the city with me?"

"I think I'll stay here if you don't mind. I need to think."

"Of course, I should be back in a few hours."

Marie is alone in Braun's house, except for the maid, the cook, and the butler, of course, but they have a way of staying invisible and Marie is grateful for the time alone and grateful there are others in the house. She still feels vulnerable even though the HHPS is all but defunct, its members in jail. The events of the last few weeks are still on her mind. Sitting by the portrait which is now back in its place above the mantel, she wills it to speak to her. *Tell me, why do you look so distressed?* Marie is tired, the stress of Colette's visit and the questions regarding the painting and brooch are weighing on her. She tilts her head back and naps as the morning sun hides behind the gathering clouds.

Marie's sleep is not restful, she is dreaming she is being chased by someone. The grandfather clock in the living room chimes loudly. The sound wakes Marie with a start. A soft rain is pelting the windows, the room is dark. Marie stokes the fire and turns on the lamp by the couch. As she does so, it dawns on her, something she hasn't thought about in a long time. The letter Evangeline left with her will. Marie had put it away, thinking the right time to read it would come naturally, no need to rush. Marie bounds up the stairs to their bedroom and retrieves her bag from the armoire. The letter is neatly tucked into the zipper pouch of her bag. She lifts it out and heads back downstairs to the fire. She settles herself and decides it not too early for a whiskey. Marie holds the letter to her chest. After all this time, will she still weep at the sight of Evangeline's handwriting? She slowly opens the letter and unfolds it; two pages.

My dear, Meine Liebe, if you are reading this, I am gone. There is so much I want you to know, but most importantly, know that I loved you more than life itself. I never found the right moment to tell you I was your real mother. The whole sorted story seemed too much to burden you with. And, you know me, I never liked to dwell on the past, and nothing mattered more to me than your happiness. I'm sorry I never told you, I hope you can forgive me, I hope your heart is happy knowing you and I are mother and daughter. Oh, Marie, I wish I did not have to leave you!

When you go to Budapest, and I know you will, you must go to the Hungarian National Museum, seek out a man named, Braun Illes. I knew his father, Josef, who was a horrible man, but Braun is not like him. The Illes family knows our history, and I believe Braun can be trusted. This is the other secret I have kept from you. You and I are decedents of the great Ludwig van Beethoven. I know it seems impossible and you may think I am stark raving mad, but it is true.

There is so much more to tell you and to be honest, it may not be safe for you to be in Budapest, but I know the Illes family, I know Braun will protect you. There are letters from the Immortal Beloved and Beethoven, there are eighteen in all, and they must be kept hidden. She is our sister, dear Marie, we are sworn to protect her secret, please, I beg you no matter how angry you are at me, please do this. You must also meet Ivan Karoly, he was my one true love, Meine Liebe, he will lead you to the letters, you can trust him. He and his friend Viktor were my dearest friends.

I am too weak to write more now but Marie, my dear love, please believe me when I say I never meant to hurt you. I loved you as no mother has ever loved her child. Be happy, Marie, live happily, follow your heart. Remember, not everything in this life can't be explained, not everything will make sense. Follow your heart, know I am with you, watching over you.

Protect her, protect Beethoven's secret, and find love. You will understand my story, her story, when you do.

All my love,

Your loving mother, Evangeline

With her mother's letter in hand, a woman she only recently learned was her real mother, Marie stares at the painting of the Immortal Beloved, a woman whose identity is unknown. But the woman looks exactly like her mother, like her; a woman her mother called, "our sister." Marie risked her life to make sure her letters and the truth of her relationship to Beethoven were kept hidden from the world, even before she read her mother's letter asking her to do so. The Immortal Beloved's expression has changed. Her eyes are softer, her face is now serene.

The voice of the Broadwood gently calls to Marie.

"You are home."

Marie smiles sipping whiskey by the fire in Braun's living room. Among the things that don't make sense and the things that cannot be explained, the artifacts of her life lay before her, the painting, her mother's letter, the brooch, and time.

THE END